D1713951

MOTHER TRUCKER

BECAUSE IT'S NEVER TOO LATE!

MISSY RYCKMAN

authorHOUSE®

AuthorHouse™
1663 Liberty Drive
Bloomington, IN 47403
www.authorhouse.com
Phone: 833-262-8899

Published by AuthorHouse 06/15/2021

ISBN: 978-1-6655-2690-6 (sc)
ISBN: 978-1-6655-2689-0 (hc)
ISBN: 978-1-6655-2691-3 (e)

Library of Congress Control Number: 2021910499

Print information available on the last page.

CONTENTS

Part 2

Part 3

ACKNOWLEDGMENTS

I dedicate this book to all my fellow truckers. You make a difference. Without you, America stops!

In loving memory of Jay Fick; your encouragement and optimism gave me hope and excitement for this industry. You are not forgotten.

Stephanie, my rock and the best Mother-Trucking friend on the road, you get me, even on bad days.

Ashley, my old soul, keep on trucking, work on that road rage, and stay away from animal shelters!

Iva, your inner beauty matches your outer beauty. I'm thankful to have met you.

Tristen, keep on trucking. Don't give up on this journey. It's in your blood.

Dana, thank you for your friendship and daily laughter. You brighten my life.

Sarah, may the world see your talents, far and wide.

Jennifer, Shannon, and Sharon, thank you for the encouragement & eagle eyes.

Mommy Jo and Daddy Jo, you made the foundation on which I stand every day.

And finally to my family, without you, I wouldn't be the woman that I am today. I love you with all my heart.

To all the others whom I have met along this journey, hammer down and always keep the rubber down and the shiny side up!

Thank you,

Melissa

PART 1

CHAPTER 1

THE RUT

A sense of dread hit her in the face like a hot skillet of grits. So far, she had only opened her eyes when her alarm had gone off, and it was only a Tuesday. None of the customers better roll his or her eyes at her today—not even one—or call her the name that she used on her dog when she would run off a few days every month. Just getting dressed was a chore these days. She couldn't shake this feeling—ever. This was her life.

On the way to the office as she sat in traffic, her mind wandered, as usual. *One of these days*, she thought. *What about one of these days?* They were her days, and she was stuck in a rut. This rut was supposed to be her calling and place in this world. All she wanted to do was throat punch the next smart-mouthed punk who disrespected her daily. She was forty-five years old. She had sat behind a desk and managed people and property for years. All she had to show for it was a hundred extra pounds and a desire to strangle stupid people. She was desperate to run away and pretend that this wasn't her life.

This was her life. She longed to go back to a time when she was happy. "Honk! Honnnkkk!" She blinked and realized that she was daydreaming and traffic was moving. She looked in her rearview mirror, and she was ready to give an apologetic wave, but she only saw an asshole flipping her off.

Oh, it's on like Donkey Kong, she thought. She moved forward and forgot the apology entirely. The impatient driver zoomed around her.

"I eat shits like you for breakfast!" he screamed at her.

"He eats shit for breakfast? Well that explains his overall shitty demeanor," she said out loud and slowed down so he didn't clip her bumper. "Just because the world is full of assholes, it doesn't mean you have to be one!" Sandy hollered, knowing he couldn't hear a word of it.

A light bulb went off in her head. Wow! It was the first creative thought she'd had in a month—maybe in years. *Maybe, I should make that into a slogan and put in on a T-shirt*, she thought. *Better yet, I could print out thousands and cram one down the throat of every asshole that is an asshole to me. Man, I'm on a roll today.* She giggled. She cracked a smile. It made her face feel weird.

As she parked her car, she took a deep breath and braced herself. Once inside her workplace, she rushed past her coworkers and shut the door to her office before anyone could make eye contact or fire off a question. *Eyes shut. Breathe. In through the nose. Out through my freaking teeth. Isn't that how it goes?* she wondered, as Molly bravely opened her door and peeked inside.

Barely seeing Molly through the slits in her eyes, Sandy said, "Yes, yes, no, I don't know. Why, who said I said yes? No, maybe next week, go ahead, and ask Fred."

"But I haven't even asked any questions yet," Molly squeaked, as Sandy opened her eyes.

"Okay, fine. What are the questions?"

"Can Dave start on the South Haven house today?"

"Yes."

"Will Jimmy be working in Dover today?"

"Yes."

"Can the Petersons wait and pay next week?"

"No."

"When will we order new T-shirts?"

"I don't know. Why, who said I said yes? Are we seeing a pattern yet Molly?"

Molly rolled her eyes. Sandy noticed, but didn't even bother saying anything. It wouldn't do any good. Those eyes would roll regardless of reprimand. She stood up; sucked in all the niceness she could muster, and went out to face the masses.

Be nice, she said, scolding herself before even walking out of her office. *Be sweet? Yeah, right, good luck with that one!* She snorted.

"Did you just snort?" Tammy asked, as Sandy rounded the corner

"Huh? No, umm, I felt a cough coming on." *Phew, quick save*, she thought.

The day trudged on, like every other one did, with clients, contractors, visitors, paperwork, phone calls, approvals, scheduled meetings, ass chewings, and the chewing of asses. It was the same old shit. It was a different day, month, and year, but the same shit. That part, the mindless repetition, hit her in the stomach, and she felt that particular feeling she got when her ulcer flared up.

She got into her car. She drove home, as usual. It was the same traffic jam. She was going a different direction, and it was a different day, but it was the same traffic. She wondered where she had gone wrong in her life. She was supposed to be happy, successful, comfortable, and all those other adjectives that are supposed to signal a sign of happiness, contentment, and the other hallmarks of a fulfilled life. Yet here she was, forty-five, fat, frumpy, mean, and—

"Honk! Honk!"

Oh my God, again? Sandy thought as she looked up and saw the same guy, same truck, same middle finger, and same asshole. This time, instead of an apology, she stepped on the gas. "Eat my dust, asshole!" she yelled. All four windows were rolled up, so she knew that he hadn't heard a word of it. *I'll think more when I get home*, she thought, as she puts distance between her and Mr. Road Rager.

Sandy made it the rest of the way home without incident, her car intact, her temper in check, and her feelings about her life still disquieted. She needed something. *What is that something? Where is that something?* she thought.

This feeling of discontentment had been swirling around inside her for a long time. The older she got, the worse it got. It had become especially worse since the kids had grown up and moved away. Her life and attention had encompassed those mini humans. They had needed her. She had needed them. She had watched her tribe grow from children, to resilient teenagers, to self-sufficient adults. They no longer needed her (as much). But she wondered if she still needed them.

But now there was this emptiness and this … what was this feeling? She couldn't put her finger on it. It was a sense of not being fulfilled, loneliness, and no meaning in life. She wondered what *had* become of her life.

Sandy remembered all the fun she used to have. Yes, all that fun had revolved around her children and family. *But that's the way it's supposed to be, isn't it? Isn't it supposed to be about family, kids, their activities, and their lives? she thought.* There were ball games, dance recitals, 4-H meetings, school plays, and other endless school activities. She hauled every kid to the fair, on vacation, on camping trips, to the mountains, and to the beach.

There were all the pictures, the fun stuff, and the things that she had to drag out just to make them happy. Of course, that's what parents were supposed to do, right?

All of a sudden, she was alone—alone alone. She didn't know what to do. She felt empty inside. She didn't quite know what the answer was. Her life consisted of work, housework, sleep, and not much else, or at least it felt that way. Her career wasn't what she needed it to be. She struggled just to get out of bed each day and make it to the office.

She didn't even know what the question was. Hold on a minute. She knew exactly what the answer was: a rut. As soon as she thought of the word, it at all came together. *This is it,* she thought. *I'm stuck in a dead-end rut.*

But what in the world was she going to do about it? That was the million-dollar question to be answered.

***

After a long unproductive day, she thought that a hot shower would give her the relaxation that she needed to fall asleep. Hoping against hope that sleep would graciously overtake her, she lay there and stared at the ceiling fan, to no avail. She watched it twirl round and round, until finally, she reached for the remote.

Maybe some old reruns will put me out. I mean, really, what is worse than watching TV at night? Sandy thought. It's not like she had anything exciting in her life. She grimaced. Channel surfing, she stopped on an old *Sanford and Son* rerun, which was one of her favorites.

She hadn't watched this episode in years, and she was tickled at the son and old man bickering at breakneck speed.

She was about to doze off when a commercial came on and the sound of a tractor-trailer's horn caught her attention. She opened her eyes when a female voice came over the TV. "What's your life like right now? What's your path in life? Have you ever thought about traveling this beautiful country *and* getting paid to do so?" the smooth and resplendent sounding woman said. All the while, a beautiful and glorious female trucker in awesome lady-trucker gear rambled down the road with her arm pumping the air horn as kids stood on the side of the road pumping their fists.

"In the ever-changing world of trucking, our company is no longer just a man's world. If you're looking for something exciting and want to be part of a growing company and industry, give us a call!"

Intrigued, she sat up in bed. What in the world had she just seen—a lady trucker? Sure, there were women truckers out there, but weren't they as rough, and road-rashed, and tougher than buzzards eating road kill? The lady on TV was beautiful, normal, and so happy. She looked like she was having fun. She looked like she was enjoying herself. The lady made it seem like it wasn't a dead-end job to her.

She thought that it was funny that she had never noticed watching a trucking commercial on TV before. Yet here she was being down on herself, moody, depressed, and in a rut big-time. She didn't know exactly what was wrong with her life. Then this happened. Was it a coincidence? Was it some sort of sign from above? *Sweet baby Jesus, are you trying to tell me something? Is this an epiphany? Maybe.*

She had been stuck in a rut just as the commercial had aired. Maybe it was speaking to her soul. Better yet, she felt like it had rocked her to the core. Her brain felt like it was electrified. So many emotions were going on inside her. But it was a good kind of emotion, which was a rarity these days.

At some point, she fell asleep. When she did, she had a smile on her face.

Sandy woke up in a better mood than she had been in for a long time. She didn't know what the difference was, but something was different. She couldn't put her finger on it, but she knew that she had dreamt of something and that it had somehow made her feel a little bit happy and maybe even content.

As she drove to work, she thought that it might help her mood throughout the entire day. Her impatient friend from the day before was thankfully not on the road. Like clockwork, traffic was backed up on the interstate. She sat there with cars around her five rows deep as they crawled along. Smiling, she thought of all the cars as snails that were lined up and ready to invade an abundant garden.

But this morning, she noticed something: a female trucker. *How odd,* she thought. *How is it I've never noticed this before? Has my head been stuck in the mud?*

The woman was fortyish and a brunette. She wore big sunglasses and a one-ear headset with a microphone bent close to her mouth. She was having a lively conversation as they sat in standstill traffic.

I wonder how long she's been driving a truck, Sandy thought. She wanted to honk at her because she felt an odd connection to this woman trucker. But she realized that she would look like an idiot if she did.

Traffic started moving. She refocused and turned her attention to the road.

Her office work went smooth for a Wednesday and she was grateful for that. *It's nothing like the anxiety I had yesterday, thank God,* she thought. She was about to shut down her computer and close the office when Shawn, the mail delivery guy, came in with the afternoon mail.

As she signed for several packages, she asked, "Hey, Shawn, let me ask you a really stupid question."

"Okay, Sandy. What's that?" Shawn replied.

"How many women drivers does your company have?"

"I don't know. I can find out, and that's not a stupid question at all. Why? You thinking about driving a truck?" Shawn grinned, picturing pretty Sandy behind the wheel of an 18-wheeler.

Sandy looked out her office doorway to see if any sets of ears where close by and then closed the door. "You know, Shawn, until last night, I never even thought about women driving trucks. Then I saw a commercial, and now that's all I can think about. It's been on my mind all day. I know women have been in the industry for years, but this may be the missing link that my life needs," Sandy said and then grinned.

"I can look into it for you if you want me to," Shawn offered.

Sandy waved her hand and said, "No, no, I'll look into it myself. Thanks for letting me pick your brain."

"Pick it anytime," Shawn teased and winked as he walked out of her office with the outgoing mail.

Sandy arrived home late as usual. Traffic had poked along. She counted five female drivers this time, among the hundred or so male drivers along her route home, not that she had paid much attention to the driver of any semi-truck until then. Now that her mind was tuned in to this, she couldn't help noticing every truck and truck driver that passed her.

She wondered why she hadn't noticed these huge trucks before. They were big and different types. She was sure that the different acronyms stood for different companies. Hell, she couldn't remember the name of the one from the commercial the other night. She'd remember it if she saw it again. She was sure of that. But could she remember it off the top of her head? Nope, nada, it wasn't happening. She felt kind of stupid. In a world as busy and big as the one she lived in, she really didn't notice the truckers on the road that much. Yes, they were always in traffic with her, they were ubiquitous, and they had the brand names of major grocery or retail stores on them, but she hadn't paid much attention to them.

She remembered watching *Smokey and the Bandit* as a kid. She had giggled with her cousins at the sheriff when he couldn't catch the good guys. She also remembered how pretty Sally Field had been back in those days. Who was she kidding? Sally Fields was still one of the prettiest women and her favorite actors of all times—besides Melissa McCarthy, of course. Everyone knew that Sandy loved Melissa McCarthy. Most people said that she favored her in looks and comedic gestures.

After fixing supper and doing a few chores, Sandy settled in for the evening and began searching online for trucking companies with high percentages of women drivers. Within seconds, it appeared at the top of the search results like a beacon that was welcoming her to come and join the team immediately: MARI TRUCKING. Her heart skipped a beat. It was the company from the late-night commercial that had struck a chord in her heart. She had found it, or it had found her. She knew that this was the missing piece that her life needed. She had never felt like this about her current job.

The MARI TRUCKING website was chock full of the latest industry, recruiting, and employment information: keywords, locations, and divisions. It even had an exclusive club for female drivers, who were called the Highway Diamonds. There were testimonials of women leaving other careers to enter the trucking industry. Some were nurses, accountants, teachers, and banking executives.

Their stories were fascinating. Strong-minded women led the industry. Women helped women. Women empowered women. Women of all colors and ages looked as if they had been trucking all their lives. For all Sandy knew, they had!

After hours of reading, she was ready for bed. She would read more later—much more. She had so much more research to do. She knew what she would be doing all weekend. She also knew for certain that she was going to join the team. She didn't know when or how, but it was going to happen. She was sure of it.

CHAPTER 2

THE DECISION

Suddenly, she felt energized. She hadn't felt like that in years. It was exhilarating and exciting.

She talked to many people, took many notes, and read many reviews. She joined several online groups. She asked a ton of questions. She browsed websites. She downloaded app after helpful app.

She reached out to her good friend Rosie, who was a truck driver herself. She had met Rosie several years ago; they had met and hit it off, on the day their sons graduated from basic training at Fort Jackson in South Carolina. They had kept in touch through the years. Rosie had a plethora of trucking knowledge. Two years earlier, she had quit her factory job to go to trucking school. She said it was the best thing she had ever done in her life.

After weeks of research and lots of prayer, she looked up the recruiter's number. Sandy made the call.

***

After what seemed like a blur of recruitment, paperwork, resignations, and storage arrangements, Sandy was set. Letters were emailed to corporate. She found a wonderful retired woman to board her dogs with. Her weekly boarding rate was affordable, and Sandy felt like she was sending Oreo and Bella off to summer camp. That was the easy part.

Telling her family, friends, and coworkers was almost comical. If her life was a movie, Melissa McCarthy would of course play her part, and it would have gone something like this:

"So, everyone, I've gathered you all together for an announcement," at a hastily thrown together cookout for family, friends, and coworkers. Of course, Sandy was dressed to the hilt, with her hair falling in glorious waves. She knew that she was going to surprise everyone. She may have overdressed for such an announcement, but to her, this was the beginning of a new direction in life, and she was excited. Her current look reflected that.

But she was nervous nonetheless. She gnawed at her fingernails, which were already nubs, and her fingernail polish was spotty at best. She kept tucking her hair behind her ears and constantly reapplying lip balm like it was going out of style. Butterflies were generating by the millions in her stomach. She hadn't been this excited in years, and she was sure that they would think she was crazy. She stared out at everybody who had gathered at the park. All eyes stared back and her.

Her breath caught in her throat, and suddenly, her mouth was as dry as a cotton ball. After all these years of white-collar-banking hours of existence, would her people understand her epic decision?

She blurted out, "I'm going to be a truck driver!"

Everyone was silent (Family, coworkers, friends, and nosy strangers whom she didn't even know). She heard very loud crickets. She saw blank stares.

Then her sons gave her big toothy grins.

"Yep. A truck driver," Sandy slowly repeated. More crickets.

Finally her mom smiled and said, "Well, this doesn't surprise me. You were always my free spirit." Sandy smiled. She knew her mom would understand her.

"Really?" said her dad. "Are you sure you can drive a big rig?"

"Well no, Dad, I don't know, but you know I'm going to try, and I won't stop 'til I get it!"

"I'm proud of you, Mom!" her daughter said. "You will rock it!"

Sandy beamed with pride. Her kids and family made her feel so proud. She hoped she wouldn't let them down.

"Well, you guys know I've been in a rut for a long time. I have been feeling lost, and I didn't know what, how, or why. Now I feel like I have a calling and a purpose. This industry needs women, and I've found a company that caters to and helps women like me achieve this goal that I have set for myself. I have done all my research, and I found a recruiter. I have sent my resignation letter in to corporate. I found a sweet lady to take care of Oreo and Bella until I finish my training, and I have a yard service taking care of my yard while I'm in training. So, does anyone have any questions?" Sandy asked, as if she were teaching a class.

Questions came from every direction. "Who will teach you?"

"A certified CDL instructor will teach me everything I need to know to get my CDL. They call the first phase MSD, and it varies on how long this phase lasts. MSD stands for MARI student driver. All students have different levels of experience, but the recruiter told me the average time for MSD took two to four weeks."

"So who will train you?"

"Another driver with the company. I'll stay on the road with that person for thirty thousand miles. That portion is called TNT. That stands for trainer and trainee."

"Will it be a man or woman?"

"I don't know, but I prefer it to be a woman. I want to see how women do it. Men have it easy. They have been doing this for decades. I want a woman's perspective, you know?"

"How much will you get paid?"

"That's for me to know and you to find out, nosy." Sandy teased her son. He always could get a rise out of her. She laughed.

"Will you blow your horn for me?"

"You betcha!" Sandy exclaimed, as she pumped her fist in the air. Her boys cupped their hands around their mouths and made the sound of a big rig's air horn. The whole group burst into laughter.

"How are you going to see over the steering wheel?"

"Really, Frank? That's the best question you got?" Sandy shook her head but laughed. Leave it to Frank, her sarcastic neighbor, to bring her short stature into the equation. "For your information," she said, "there are women shorter than me that drive semi-trucks every day, thank you very much. I'm sure I will not have a problem." *At least, I hope I don't*, she thought.

"Will you wear a trucker hat?" Only a daughter would worry about her fashion accessories.

"Maybe I will, maybe I'm won't! We'll just have to see, won't we?" Sandy smiled.

Despite their rapid-fire nature, the questions weren't that hard to answer. Sandy answered each question in a resounding manner. Sandy wasn't one who would just fly off on a whim without doing thorough research and making sound decisions. No one seemed baffled by her decision to completely change careers in midlife. In just a few short weeks, she was going to do just that—change everything she knew: her career, lifestyle, and maybe even her love life. She agreed that it could always use a jolt. Sandy laughed to herself. *Let the fun begin*, she thought.

CHAPTER 3

THIS IS IT!

What have I gotten myself into? she thought, as she giggled somewhere between Alabama and Mississippi. At least, she *thought* that's where she was. At this point, she had lost track of time, the day, and the night. All she knew was that it was stinky and that the bus ride was the longest one of her life. She hoped that her luggage was still in the storage area beneath her and that she would arrive in Springfield as planned the next morning.

All of her hopes and dreams were in the seat with her. Without a shower or a toothbrush and having consumed just a small bag of chips and a Coke since the day before, she was worried that she would second-guess almost everything. Sleep would surely solve everything, if she could get to that point.

All she wanted was a hot shower, her feet on the pavement, oh, and to see Springfield. Her new life awaited her. Her old life was gone and dead. It had been dead for a long time. She just hadn't known it until that wonderful night when she had felt reborn. New life had been breathed back into her soul, all because of a simple commercial—and a trucking commercial at that.

Her life could be summed up like a Lifetime movie, minus Valerie Bertinelli and her child-snatching drama. Her life had been boring and stagnate. She had never seemed to be motivated. She hadn't been happy in the least or able to figure out the reason why.

She had done everything that she was supposed to do, or perhaps, she had done the things that she thought being successful consisted of. Everything she had done up until this point made her *look* successful. But being successful didn't bring happiness, not anymore.

She had raised three beautiful, successful children. She was a wonderful daughter. At least, she hoped that her parents thought she was. She had had the career she was supposed to have: white collar, office job, banker hours, weekends offs, boring commute, cookie-cutter house, and typical thirty-year mortgage. It was the typical American-dream life. "Boring" is what she called. She had had no life. She repeated that again in her head: "I had no life."

She had had no life until now. She was hours and a couple of states away, and soon, she would be in training for a new career and a new life. It was not only for a new job but also for a new life.

***

Sandy had spent the last month pouring over every article, website, and YouTube video that she could find. Hard work was ahead of her. She wasn't afraid of getting her hands dirty, or at least, she didn't think so.

She'd sat in an office for so long, she was almost afraid she wouldn't be able to keep up. But she knew she wouldn't give up. This was now going to be her life. She knew that people from all walks of life lived on the road: big, small, fat, and skinny. Sure, she was fat, but so were a lot of truckers. She could do this. She knew it.

Her biggest worry was the physical fitness test. She'd spent the last few weeks walking a little bit further every night. She didn't want to embarrass herself when it came time for the test. This was her only worry.

"Welcome to Tennessee," the sign read, as the bus eased on down the road. *Getting closer,* she thought, as she shifted in her seat, closed her eyes, and tried to sleep a little more. But sleep was not so easy to come by. The sounds and smells made sure of that, and her brain absolutely would not shut off. She always said that she had a live hamster on a wheel in her head, and the damn thing ran twenty-four hours a day. Even as exhausted as she was, Herby was up there in her head, running on that damned wheel.

After two more states, she would be there, and her training would start. Her new life would start. She was so excited. She had been studying for her permits and tests because she wanted to make sure she passed the first time, every time. Failure was not an option. She had too much riding on this. She had given up almost everything, but to her, it was worth it.

She now had a purpose. She hadn't even made it to her destination, and she already felt like she was part of an elite group. She was one of *them*. Okay, so she wasn't one *yet*. But she was going to be one soon. With every breath in her body, she would give it her all. She was ready. She had done her research, she had started working out, and she wasn't going to let this chance pass her by.

She must have fallen asleep because she was suddenly awakened by passengers around her, who were getting up and rushing past her seat. She stood slowly because she was stiff from the long ride. Finally, she was in Springfield, Missouri. She was there.

The butterflies came back with a vengeance. She shuffled off the bus with the masses and then tried to collect her luggage. Luckily, she had packed smartly. She only had a large duffle bag and her brightly colored floral backpack.

The recruiter had given her the number to call for the shuttle. But she didn't need to call, the shuttle bus was already there and waiting. She found her way to the other side of the Greyhound station and to the waiting shuttle bus for MARI TRUCKING and boarded with no problem.

It was almost nine o'clock on a Sunday night, and all she wanted was a hot shower and something to eat. She realized that this had been a recurring desire throughout her trip.

She rode on the shuttle bus, stealing glances here and there of those who were also heading for new lives. The guy in front of her had tattoos covering his arms, his neck, and what she could see of his legs. His hair was pulled back into a man bun, and his ears were gauged out with holes big enough to stick her fingers through. Their eyes met, and she offered him a quick smile. He smiled back.

As she glanced down the aisle of the bus, she realized that she was the only woman there. That scared and energized her at the same time. She quickly counted fifteen guys and one Sandy.

Math was never her best subject, but she figured it was about 6 percent (She had read that MARI TRUCKING was double the national average, and it boasted a healthy 12 percent as women drivers). *Please be more women in this group*, she prayed, as the bus rolled down the road in the darkness.

The shuttle bus came to a stop in front of an older converted hotel. When the door opened, the sign read, "Campus Park." Everyone got out and lined up to get their luggage from the back of the bus. She was pleasantly surprised at the courteous nature of most of the men. Sandy was the last person in line, and the guy in front of her even handed her duffle bag to her.

"Thank you!" she said, as she grabbed the straps of the bag.

The lobby of the hotel was a flurry of activity. Luggage and people were everywhere. Road-weary people crowded around. It looked like total chaos when she walked into the lobby, but within a minute, the two guys behind the counter had everything running like a well-oiled machine. Steve and Jay calmly directed new students into the correct lines and shoed them the place to stack their luggage. *Steve and Jay are easy names to remember,* Sandy thought.

Steve and Jay took the students' money for the registration fee. They handed out hotel key cards, campus maps, food vouchers, and classroom schedules. They pointed everyone to the cooler that held boxed lunches. They did everything with such ease that it looked like they'd been doing it for years, which Sandy thought that they probably had.

Jay was funny, and his easy laugh and the twinkle in his eye seemed to calm everybody down. "It's just like shipping your kid off to boot camp," he said with a laugh, as he handed Sandy her printed forms.

"I know all about that," Sandy told him. "I sent two son off myself."

Jay smiled at her sincerely and said, "The next time you talk to your boys, tell them that I said, 'Thank you for their service!'"

Sandy smiled back, "I will definitely do that," she said.

Luggage, rucksacks, and bags of all sorts were thrown everywhere. It looked like a chaotic mess to Sandy. But to Steve and Jay, it was just a typical Sunday night.

"Place your luggage in the hallway against the wall," Steve said, "and go to the first classroom on the left."

Classes already? Sandy thought. They had just arrived, and they were tired and hungry. All Sandy wanted was a shower. It was Sunday night. Shit was about to get a real!

She quickly found a seat and looked around. The seats were filling up fast. There were so many people and so many men. She counted three other women. So far, she hadn't made eye contact with them.

Some people were people watchers, like she was. They sat back and just observed. Some seemed more road-worn than she was and slept on their folded arms. Some were the life of the party, and they acted as if they were hosting a New Year's Eve bash and the countdown would happen any minute.

Several people were gathered around one such host. He was the unmistakable ringleader. All the younger guys were hanging onto his every word. The man sitting next to the Sandy nudged her arm, cocked his head in the direction of the ringleader, and said, "I wonder if he knows how stupid he really looks."

Sandy burst out laughing. As several people glanced at her, her laughter quickly died away. "No," Sandy said, "he has no clue." *And he never will*, she thought.

All of the seats were filled, and people were beginning to line the back wall. Sandy stopped watching people, shuffled her papers, and got down to business. She was here for one reason and one reason only. She was going to become a truck driver. No, that wasn't entirely true. She was here for a new life and to become a truck driver.

The instructor that came into the class was precise and to the point. He looked like he was in his sixties, and he had a laid-back attitude. He was tall and stocky and sported a T-shirt with the company logo and a pair of faded blue jeans. He also looked like he didn't take shit off anybody. The class started immediately.

"Welcome to MARI TRUCKING. My name is Walt, and we are glad you made it. Here's your itinerary and code of conduct—what we expect. We hope you make it through the week. A lot of students call this 'hell week', and you will soon find out why. You will be responsible for every class, for every computer-based training course, for all your permits, and most importantly, to be on time. And if you fail, it's on you. I hope you all have studied, especially for the drug test."

It took several seconds before most of the people in the room realized that it was a joke. Several people looked like it wasn't a joke and they thought that it was a test that they could study for.

Sandy bit back a giggle. She realized that some people in this class might not make it through the week. *Wow*, she thought. She could not imagine going through that hellish two-and-a-half-day ride on that musty, crusty Greyhound and spending all the time that she had prepared for this moment, only to have to go back home. What a sobering thought. She had given up her old life for this. What if it didn't work out? There wasn't an answer to that question. She would make it.

With a wave of his hand, the class was dismissed, and all students were on their own. Sandy made a beeline for the cooler in the lobby. She was starvin' like Marvin, and she'd be damned if she was going to miss out even on a lousy boxed lunch, which most likely had been sitting in the cooler all day.

It was almost 11:00 p.m., and she hadn't even made it to her room yet. Her intuition was correct. There were only four boxed lunches left by the time she got her greedy little hands on one. Ten people were in the line behind her. Six of them probably weren't even thinking about food. They were thinking about what a good time they would have, as if this was going to be party week at Daytona Beach, college week, or a tailgating weekend. It seemed like it was their first time away from home. Some people acted like they had never even left home alone before.

Sandy collected her duffle bag, tucked her boxed lunch into her backpack along with all of her papers, looked at her map, and walked down the winding hallways. Once she had passed the classrooms and offices, she entered the hallway leading to the hotel portion of the campus.

In the time it took to get to her room, she became drenched in sweat. Hell, Sandy sweat like a pig no matter what she did. But after lugging her duffle bag and her fat self halfway across the campus and up two flights of steps, she finally made it to her room.

The campus may have looked old, but surprisingly, the room was clean and neat. There were two full-sized beds, a small round table with one chair, a flat screen TV on top of a dresser, and a nice window AC unit blasting out cold air.

Her recruiter had told her that she would be sharing a room with another student, and Walt had informed the class of this as well. Sandy was the first one in the room, so she claimed the bed that was closest to the AC unit. *Second victory of the night*, she thought, as she tossed her duffle bag and backpack onto her bed.

She quickly washed up, pulled her boxed lunch out along with her stack of new papers, and began to read and eat the wilted but tasty turkey sandwich. She looked at her cell phone. It was already midnight, and they had to be in class by 7:00 a.m. on the next day. Her food voucher showed that breakfast started at 6:00 a.m.

She hurriedly finished her midnight snack, dug through her luggage for her toiletries' bag, and then pulled out an outfit so she'd be ready for the next morning. She quickly took a shower, secured her wet hair into a ponytail, set two alarms on her cell phone, and closed her eyes. *Hell week, here I come!* she thought.

CHAPTER 4

ORIENTATION WEEK

Her breakfast was a simple affair. She selected scrambled eggs, turkey sausage links, a biscuit with grape jelly, and the largest Mountain Dew that she could find. She knew she'd be taking her drug test later, and she didn't want to be one of *those* ladies who couldn't go on command. When the time was right, she would be ready.

The clock on the wall read 6:30 a.m. It was time to head to her first class, and she wasn't about to be late. She threw her trash away and headed outside. More people were outside now. Some looked like they had just gotten up, and some were bright-eyed and bushy-tailed.

In the first parking space of parking lot, a semi-truck sat with its hood open and several people standing around the engine peering inside. A group of newbies wore new neon-yellow vests. They were holding sheets of white paper and pointing to different parts of the engine. There was another group of people standing back by a small trailer, which was attached to the semi. All were talking and pointing. Sandy was excited. She wanted to be part of a group like that.

She pulled out her map, went inside, found the correct classroom, and quickly found a seat. There were rows of tables with computers on them. Headphones hung on each modem next to each monitor. She found a seat on the end of the second row and quickly took out her paper, pen, and forms.

She then settled in and did a little people watching. The two guys to her right looked like the true definition of what she thought a trucker should look like. They wore trucker hats, which had some type of company name on them. They had sideburns. One guy had a set that Burt Reynolds would have been jealous of. *Holy moly!* she thought. The other guy had a set of muttonchops and looked eerily like Chris Farley. He even laughed like him. Both sported faded trucking T-shirts and Wrangler jeans. Both looked like they had been truckers for years and this wasn't their first rodeo.

Both guys were talking to another guy, who was in front of them. He looked completely different. He had light skin, long wavy hair, a button-down polo shirt, and khakis. He looked more like an administrative executive than a trucker. He was animated and excited like Sandy was. He was asking Mutton and Chops question after question. Mutton and Chops were fielding the questions like professionals.

Sandy tried not to appear too obvious, but the guy had some good questions. She stopped and listened. Before she knew it, class was about to begin.

A guy her age, who was somewhat on the stocky side, in the company's polo, and wearing designer jeans that were complete with rhinestones on the pockets, came walking down the center aisle. If her grandmother were alive today, she would've said he had on glitter britches. His name was Jamie, and he commanded the room. He looked like he could have been a distant cousin of one of the Duck Dynasty boys. He had a long beard, short hair, and a baseball cap with the company logo embroidered on it.

Jamie didn't waste any time starting the orientation. It was a whirlwind of activity. Jamie began the class by welcoming everyone to the company. He told everybody that the next several months were like one big job interview. He went on to describe all of the basic company jargon and to go through the week's itinerary. He quickly broke the class up into four groups, and Sandy was part of the *A* group.

The *A* group was in the first to do the physical test. They immediately left the conference room and shuffled toward a room down the hall, where they stood in line. She couldn't see into the room because the line had already snaked out into the hallway. She and her little, fat, short self worried about this the most. Yes, she knew she wasn't the fattest in the class or the shortest. She just didn't want to be the one who failed. The line slowly moved into the room.

As the line made its way toward the doorway, she got her first glimpse of what the physical test consisted of. There was a long table with several young women in company polos writing information down as students shuffled by the table. There was a ladder on the wall. Weights were on the floor, and tarps were on racks of shelves taller than Sandy was. The butterflies returned to Sandy's stomach with a vengeance, but she had a good feeling that she was going to pass it.

Sandy shuffled in, gave the girls her full name, and moved through the different stations. She climbed the ladder until her head touched the ceiling. She heaved a twenty-pound kettle bell up to her chest five times in a row. She was told, "Light weight. Heavy. Heavier. Stand on your toes. Bend at the waist. Arms up. Arms out." She was waiting for someone to blurt out *Simon says*, and she bit back a giggle.

Then she started to sweat. One thing that Sandy was known for was sweating profusely. She was in a cold room, doing minimal physical exertion, yet she looked like she was in a triathlon, finishing up the twenty-five mile biking portion of the race. She moved on to the tarp-lifting station, and they asked if she planned on going to the flatbed division. "No," she said and hoped that she didn't look as pitiful as she sounded.

She made it to the last station, which was the kneeling portion. She had to kneel on one knee and stand up without assistance. She was worried. She went down on one knee, suddenly feeling like Colin Kaepernick, and began to giggle. As soon as she began to giggle, she felt like peeing her pants, which made her giggle more. This caused her to shift off balance and almost fall over.

The guy conducting the tests was freakishly tall and looked at her with concern, saying, "Are you okay?"

"Yes," Sandy said, heaving and biting back a giggle. She wobbled some more.

She was about to touch the floor with her hands to steady herself, when the instructor (Sandy aptly nicknamed him *Too Tall Jones* in her head) barked at her, "No hands on the ground! You must get up unassisted!"

Geez Luweez, Sandy thought. *Fatty here is just trying to un-kaepernick herself while trying not to pee by putting a few fingers on the floor for moral support, and Major Too Tall Jones thinks she's trying to cheat already.*

"Okay", Sandy exclaimed, "I've got this!" She put her hands on her knee, wobbled like the glorious thick chick that she knew that she was and stood up. All these other people were doing the easiest physical fitness test of their lives. Then here was Sandy. Yes, she knew this was going to be a personal struggle. The hard stuff hadn't even begun, but she was doing it, pig sweat and all. Her black capri leggings were already sticking to her calves. Sweat soaked the back of her neck, and her bangs were dripping wet. She stood there grinning like a stupid idiot. She had passed the test.

With properly initialed paperwork in hand, she moved on to the next obstacle: the drug-screening test. How hard could that be? As she walked out the door drenched in sweat and looking like a hot mess, she made eye contact with several people.

"I didn't know the test was gonna be that hard?" she heard one girl whisper to another.

"Ah, it was nothing," Sandy said as she wheezed and strolled by the women. She was trying to look more poised then she felt. "You've got this is!" Sandy yelled and pumped her fist in the air, as the entire back end of the line burst into laughter.

CHAPTER 5

WAIT! DON'T GO!

The drug screening was being conducted in the women's bathroom of the classroom building. The line for the bathroom was all the way down the hallway and around the corner. All the fit and trim students who had breezed through the previous test were already looking bored.

Sandy got in line, and that's when her bladder decided that it was time to go. The people in line slowly shuffled forward, and one by one, they came out of the restroom with their urine cups in hand. The two white-coated technicians moved everyone along efficiently, but Sandy's poor little bladder was screaming.

By the time it was finally her turn, she felt like Forrest Gump in the scene with John F. Kennedy and the fifteen Dr. Peppers. White Coat Number One handed her a cup, told her to go into the middle stall, do her business, and not to flush when she was finished.

Sandy glanced at the stalls and realized that the middle stall was made for little people. She was pretty sure her thighs would touch the walls. Her claustrophobia raised its ugly head suddenly. *Oh, this is gonna be fun*, she thought. Crammed in the middle stall, Sandy opened the cup and balanced it on top of the toilet paper holder. She was still hot and sweaty from the previous challenge, and her panties and leggings were sticking to her like thick glue.

In the mist of yanking her pants down and off her sweaty thighs, her capris stuck to her legs, and her bladder decided it couldn't wait any longer, so she proceeded to go. *No, no, no, no, hold up!* Sandy mentally screamed at herself, as she rushed to grab the cup and tried to catch the pee in midstream. Poor Sandy was drenched in sweat, hovered over the toilet, had her leggings stuck at mid-thigh, had her arm awkwardly underneath her leg, and knew that most of her pee hadn't made it anywhere near the cup. She pulled the cup up to look at it, and sure enough, there was barely enough pee to cover the bottom of the cup. "Dammit!" Sandy said. "What am I going to do?" She quickly finished her business, and with a look of shame on her face, she told White Coat Number One, "I missed the cup!"

White Coat Number One looked at Sandy without saying a word. Then she walked out and whispered into White Coat Number Two's ear. Sandy did not know what they were talking about, but she was mortified. White Coat Number Two takes her to the side and says, "Okay, here's what we have to do. You will have two hours to produce another sample. You will get forty ounces of water to drink as well. If you do not produce another sample, you will be disqualified for failing to produce a clean sample."

Great. I've gotta sit here and look like a dunce, Sandy thought. A chair was brought in and placed next to the opening of the bathroom. They might as well have placed a neon sign above her head explaining her issue. Another student appeared with two large cups of water for her to drink. Sandy sat down, closed her eyes, and began to drink. *Oh, my God, this is so embarrassing*, she thought, as she gulped the water down. They might as well have put a big-ass neon flashing sign above her head that said, "Fat chick in skinny stall and sweaty yoga pants missed the pee cup." She was sure everyone in line knew exactly what had happened, and she felt like crawling under the tiny chair that she was sitting on.

Other students came and went, and still Sandy sat there like a bump on a log. Of all times for her bladder to go dark, this would be the time. One hour and fifteen minutes later, she asked if she could try again. White Coat Number One gave her another cup. This time, her pants did not stick, but she did not produce enough for the test. *Dammit x 401.012!* Sandy's brain screamed.

She went out to face the music. She sat back down, and White Coat Two said, "You now have forty-five minutes. If you cannot produce enough volume for our test, you will be sent home and disqualified." Those words hit her like a punch to the stomach. She suddenly felt sick.

She was *not* going home because of sticky yoga pants and a bursting bladder that couldn't wait for the cup. She closed her eyes and shut out the world. She was so embarrassed. Then she heard the same speech that she was given. "You can't go either?"

She opened her eyes and saw a guy who must have been in the same boat that she was in.

"Nah," Sandy giggled. "I missed the cup entirely." He had a strange look on his face, and she quickly said, "Fat girl problems. You wouldn't understand." He laughed, and several people within earshot did also.

All of a group of *A* and most of group *B* had finished the drug-screening portion, when Sandy made her final trip to the middle stall. With cup in hand and a sincere prayer to sweet baby Jesus, she tried again. This time, her yoga pants didn't stick, and Sandy was able to produce half a cup of pee. *Dear Lord, please let this be enough*, she prayed. She quickly went out, and with pleading eyes, she said, "Please tell me this is gonna be enough."

White Coat One said, "Well, let's check." She tested the liquid's temperature and then poured the urine into three vials. The third vial had just enough pee and not a drop more.

Success, sweet success, she thought. Sandy closed her eyes, and her heart skipped a beat. She had done it. She walked out, pumped her fist in the air, and said, "That's what I'm talking about." Everybody laughed. Who knew that peeing in a cup could be so damn hard?

CHAPTER 6

AND THE DOCTOR SAYS

As Sandy trudged down the hallway, she looked at the long list that she needed to get done. She had just wasted three hours because of a little bathroom stall, clingy yoga pants, and a pee cup. But she had been victorious in the face of struggle, and nothing was stopping her now.

As she looked at the long line for the doctor's office, her stomach grumbled. Her stomach won the battle, and she went through the door across from the doctor's office, which led to the cafeteria. As she entered the room, she locked eyes with several people from the *A* group. *Great*, she thought. She sheepishly smiled as one of them clapped.

"Glad to see you made it," one funny group-*A* comrade teased.

Sandy bowed, rolled her hand forward comically, and said, "Thank ya. Thank ya very much," she said, as she curled her lip curled in perfect Elvis fashion. She quickly stepped in line, grabbed a tray, and blended in nicely. Lunch was a quick and easy fifteen-minute blur.

Then Sandy went to the doctor and the physical exam. She joined the line, and time ticked away. As she stood and waited, she talked to the people who were around her to pass the time. They were upbeat and excited to be there like she was. Several came from the same area of the country as she did, and a few came from the Midwest.

One girl came all the way from the tip of Florida. Hearing her Greyhound story made Sandy's sound as if she had glided in on a parade float. The guy behind her had a different story. It was his second time coming there. He explained that he had needed to go home to get some kind of medical release from his doctor. So he had to take a Greyhound home, get the required doctor's statement, and start all over. *Geez*, Sandy thought, *I hope I don't have to do that.*

When Sandy could finally see inside the room, her heart sank. There were at least forty-five people waiting in chairs. It was going to be a long day for sure.

She finally made it to the window, and she was given a clipboard with several papers. She found an empty seat and got to work. She completed the forms in record time. She listed all her medications, illnesses, and the like.

They called her name, and she jumped up. *Please don't let me screw this up*, she prayed, as she walked into the front room that had scales and a blood-pressure machine. She stepped on the scale, closed her eyes, and then peeked. She was heavier than she thought that she was, but no springs popped out, and no alarms went off. She sat down to have her blood pressure and heart rate checked.

"BP looks good," the nurse muttered. "Heart rate is a bit high though."

Great, she thought. She held her breath. She could feel her heart beating through her nostrils. *Is this helping or making it worse?* she thought. She tried meditation. *I have never meditated a day in my life, but it couldn't hurt to start, could it?*

She thought back to the day she gave birth to her second son—the son she had had naturally and with no epidural or medication. The nurse kept saying, "Remember all the Lamaze stuff." All the Lamaze stuff that she remembered was focusing on one thing, such as the pattern of any object in the room and only that object. Then she needed to listen to herself breathe. Her focal point was one piece of ugly-ass patterned wallpaper, which was directly in front of her. She concentrated on breathing slowly and steadily through the pain.

She wasn't giving birth to an eight-pound ten-ounce bundle of joy for this exam, but damn, if it didn't work. The nurse checked her heart rate again and said that she was good to go to the next station.

Next, Sandy went to have her hearing, balance, and eyes tested, including color distinction. She filled out forms for all the medications that she was taking, both prescription and over-the-counter medications. She sailed through it.

The next stop was the sleep-apnea study. Sandy had been lucky when she had been assigned a recruiter. She had been told to bring three months' worth of sleep apnea documentation. That was one of the questions she had been asked in the beginning. She had been diagnosed several years earlier. She swore by her machine. The disease ran in her family, and she religiously used it nightly.

The company who monitored her machine had emailed her a copy of her results. It was supposed to have emailed a copy to MARI TRUCKING as well. She had all her necessary documents for her CPAP machine and her original sleep-apnea study. She was thankful that her recruiter had told her to bring all of this so that it wouldn't delay her training.

Some weren't so lucky. As she sat waiting, several people were grumbling about having to be tested for sleep apnea because their BMI index was too high. One guy asked Sandy if she needed to be tested. She said that she didn't.

He rudely said, "Why not?" Several people looked over at them.

Sandy cheekily grinned and said, "Because, this *fat* chick already had her study done before she got here. I look in the mirror every day. I don't need a company to tell me I'm fat."

"Holy shit," the guy next to her said and then burst out laughing. "I guess she told you."

The girl next to Sandy patted her arm. "Girl, don't let people like him get to you."

Sandy shook her head. "I don't. If the worst thing someone is going to say about me is that I'm fat, I think I'm going to be okay in this world."

The girl fist-bumped Sandy and said, "Rock on, sista. You are going places. I just know it."

The physical exam was the easiest. It was mostly a doctor pushing and prodding, and luckily as a woman, there was no genital exam involving coughing and cupping! The discussion with the doctor about her medication and current ailments was thorough. Sandy asked detailed questions about medications that she could take or not take while on the road. She wanted to make sure that she would be in compliance at all times. Finally, the doctor's examination portion was done.

As she walked out, people were milling about. Many people looked as tired as she felt. Others looked like they were ready to party. *Who has that kind of energy? Oh yeah, all those young ones,* Sandy thought. They were young enough to be her kids and run circles around her. *They can have it,* she thought. She just wanted to sit down for a moment, regroup, and see what else she needed to do on her list for the day.

She had missed the last shuttle of the day to the DMV for her permit tests, so she went to the computer lab to watch videos and start her computer-based training. She was going to stay focused and make it through this week.

She didn't know exactly how many hours she had worked on her video assignments, but she called it a night at ten o'clock. She walked outside and toward her room. More people were outside, where it was hot and humid even for that late hour. Her back and neck were stiff from sitting, watching the videos, and answering many questions during the computer-based tests, but she had made a huge dent in the number of tests that had to be done by Thursday. Videos included company policies, safety, regulations, and lots of other things.

She wasn't alone in the computer lab. Several like-minded students wanted to get a jump on the week's work. When she walked outside, she found almost everyone else. *Ah, the procrastinators,* she mused. *I could pick any one of those long-haired hippy boys, and he could be my oldest son.* She giggled to herself. Her son was the ultimate procrastinator, and judging by half the class, he would have fit right in.

"Hey funny girl!" someone yelled.

Sandy looked up and asked, "Me?" She grinned, knowing that it was someone who had caught one of her mortifying moments of the day.

"Yeah, you!" Several people laughed at this.

While walking toward her building, Sandy turned around and walked backward, bowed, and in her best British accent said, "Good evening, ladies and gentlemen." Several people waved and laughed. *These are my people,* she thought, as she slid her hotel key card into the main door's lock to access the building. She smiled all the way to her room. That smile even touched her soul.

CHAPTER 7

IT'S ONLY TUESDAY?

Tuesday was bright and sunny, and Sandy's energy matched it. She was standing with the early birds when the cafeteria lady unlocked the door. She was going to be on the first shuttle to the DMV this morning. She was nervous, but it was a good kind of nervous. For weeks, she had been studying the different endorsements, and she prayed she wouldn't get a brain freeze.

The ride to DMV was pleasant, and Sandy got her first real view of Springfield. After all, it had been well past 9:00 p.m. when she had stepped off the Greyhound bus on Sunday. Heck, it felt like she had been there longer than only two days. She had a lot to accomplish today.

She stepped off the shuttle and walked with the others into the DMV. She rode silently in the elevator and nervously chewed on a fingernail. The door opened, and all ten passengers made a beeline for the number clicker. Half the seats were already occupied by other DMV customers. Sandy sat down holding the number "28."

She continued studying her endorsements on her phone until her number was called. "Twenty eight!" Sandy almost jumped out of her seat.

This is it, she thought. She quickly put her phone in her backpack and walked to the testing center.

After what felt like an eternity but in reality was less than forty-five minutes, Sandy walked out of the center, pumped and elated. She had passed every single endorsement the first time. She felt like doing her chubby white girl dance. But she figured that she would save that for her hotel room. She waited for her permit documents and then left the room.

She rode the elevator down the ground level and joined several people who were waiting for the shuttle to return. The mood of the group was mixed. Some had passed all their endorsements. Some had passed half and failed half. A handful of the students had failed all of them. The ones that had failed were stunned.

"I can't believe how hard those test questions were, man," one dejected rider sulked.

"Didn't you study all the endorsements?" one of the guys from the group asked.

"Study what?" the student replied.

Well, that explains it, Sandy thought.

She rode back to the campus on cloud nine. She was amped up and happy, but she remained focused. Several classes were on today's itinerary, and she did not want to be late. She got back in plenty of time and found a seat in the lobby so that she could relax for a few minutes and regroup.

The groups were all back again, and people were starting to break off into smaller groups. She sank down on a cushioned sofa next to the guy she'd made small talk with on the shuttle. He was funny like she was, and they both were people watchers.

Two days in, her favorite target was the curly headed guy from South Florida with the cabana hat, white T-shirt, open, bright, and floral-print shirt, khakis, and Chuck Taylors. Oh, and Sandy couldn't forget his skateboard. Yes, he had a skateboard. If he had been younger, it would not have been as funny to Sandy and her new friend Ramon, but this guy was older than Sandy was, and she was sure he was older than Ramon was.

Cabana Boy had been Sandy's name for him when she had watched him jump on his skateboard and push off the curb on the first night that they had arrived on campus. What made her giggle was that the parking lot was not very big. There were so many people milling about that Cabana

Boy had to stop every few feet because people were walking in front of him and getting in his way. But boy, oh boy, did Cabana Boy think he was the shit.

Maybe this was his moment to relive his youth. Maybe he was trying to impress the younger guys or the women. Sandy made eye contact with several women, and based on their knowing looks, they were in complete agreement with Sandy. Cabana Boy just looked like a moron.

She also noticed that the group was somewhat smaller than it had been yesterday. Based on gossip that she had heard in the cafeteria and on the shuttle, several people obviously hadn't studied hard enough for the drug-screening test on the day before. The thought kind of made Sandy feel sad for a moment. Then it made her feel strangely angry. *How can people knowingly lie about their drug use, spend time and company money to travel quite a distance, and just hope that they might pass a screening,* she thought. Moments like these made her turn into a momma bear. She was glad that she didn't have to worry about those issues because she had preached to her kids when they were younger and before entering the service.

Class was about to begin again, and Sandy went to find a seat. Her day was trudging right along, and she prayed that there would be no hiccups like ones from yesterday. She attended classes, went to lunch, attended more classes, filed documents, and took computer tests. The day trudged on until finally, it was Group A's turn for the simulator lab.

The simulator lab looked like a big video-arcade room, but she didn't dare call it that in front of the instructors. Sandy was given the heads-up by Ramon that Jake, the silver haired instructor, would flip his sticks if someone referred to his pride and joy as a video game.

Well, Sandy was glad to get the heads-up, but it didn't take long for Jake to flip out. It just happened to be on Cabana Boy and his little crew, who jokingly compared it to a bigger version of Grand Theft Auto, truckers' edition. Jake immediately told Cabana Boy that the simulator was his brainchild, not even close to an arcade game, and much more than that. Sandy and Ramon both had to practically hold their lips in place to keep from laughing. It was funny, but it wasn't. The look Jake gave the students made that laughter die in the back of their throats.

The system in the room was incredible. There were big screens, air-ride seats, dash panels, and steering wheels. It looked just like the interior of an actual semi.

Sandy felt nervous when it was her turn to sit in the driver's seat and buckle her seat belt. The steering wheel hummed in her hands, and the screens in front of her came alive. Everything looked so realistic. People were walking and dogs were running across the street. There were cars and other trucks. It was all so real. Sandy was enthralled.

Her fifteen minutes were up before she knew it, so she unbuckled her seat belt, and the next guy settled in. This went on until all students had had a turns. Then each person got several more chances to drive.

After class, Sandy needed some fresh air. She hadn't had a chance to put on her new neon-yellow safety vest with the company logo on it, which had been distributed that day in class. She pulled her vest out of her backpack, headed outside, and became one of many—the sea of neon yellow.

As soon as Sandy walked outside, the Missouri humidity smacked her in the face. *Great*, she thought. Pig sweat would be showing up within seconds, and she hadn't done a damn thing but walk outside.

She walked over to the semi that had its hood open. Several students were already there with papers in hand. She stood back for a moment, but then a guy motioned her closer and said, "Don't be shy, little lady."

"Little and shy are not in my vocabulary," Sandy said and laughed.

"How's your pre-trip?" the guy asked, as she unzipped her backpack to find her papers.

"Horrible," she replied. "I spent so much time studying my endorsements so that I would pass them on the first try that I haven't even looked at them." Suddenly, several eyes were on her.

"Well, did you pass on the first try?" the guy asked her.

"Heck yeah, I did," Sandy practically yelled, and the guy fist-bumped her. *My people*, she thought again and then blended in with the guys. All their heads were in the engine compartment.

After an hour of sweat, engine parts, and the proper wording that was required for each part, Sandy was ready for the cool air of the computer room and the million videos waiting to be watched, followed by a test. Only one more day of classes and tests, and orientation would be a thing of the past. She would be moving on to the next phase.

Thursday was a blur of check marks. She was in and out of classrooms and in and out of offices. She took computer-based tests. Check, check, and it was done. Sandy could feel the weight lifting off her shoulders, one check mark at a time. She was getting it done. Orientation was coming to an end, and she was ready to get her company student ID badge. She still wasn't an employee yet, but she was now ready for the next phase: MSD (MARI student driver) training.

MSD training typically took two-to-six weeks with a certified CDL instructor. The instructors would take the students out on the road and teach them everything that they needed to know to pass the Missouri State CDL Exam. She couldn't wait to call her family and tell them the exciting news.

CHAPTER 8

THE MOMENT SHE'S BEEN WAITING FOR

Friday morning, Sandy was bursting with pride when she dressed and clipped her badge on her vest. She couldn't wait to ride to the terminal and go on the tour. She watched several videos on YouTube, but nothing could prepare her for how big, spacious, and beautiful the place was.

She stepped off the shuttle and headed inside with everyone else. She stopped when she saw a little white robotic mower gliding over the grass. She stopped to take a picture. Her mom and dad would love to see it.

She walked inside, and it was like no trucking terminal she had ever envisioned. The place was enormous. There was a full-sized basketball court, fitness room, and huge spiral staircase leading to the second floor. There was a café, a company store, an embroidery shop, and an onsite day care center. Sandy was amazed. The place was buzzing with activity, even at 6:30 a.m. Office personnel wearing security badges and drivers in various degrees of dress and wakefulness all coexisted in the same space.

Lounge chairs, tables, and counters filled the entire space, and the place was hopping.

Sandy finally made it to the cafeteria and took a few minutes to decide on what to splurge on for her celebratory breakfast. Every Friday, there was a safety meeting where breakfast was free. She decided on some hash browns and biscuits with gravy. She waited for her order, made her way through the line, and found a seat with her people. Over half the class had made it to this point, and most of them had arrived on the shuttle. She hoped the rest of the class would be able to finish up all of their requirements.

Just as Sandy was finishing up her breakfast, the meeting started. The speakers were animated and jovial, and she felt at ease with such important people. The owner of the company spoke, welcomed the new students, and wished them luck. She felt like she was part of one big family. *Today was such a great day*, Sandy thought.

The meeting was soon over, and the tour began. Jamie, in dazzling jeans, led the tour. There was a hair salon, movie theater, post office, laundry facility, and bunk rooms. There were also personnel, security, dispatch, leasing, and sales offices. They went up one floor and down another, through one set of glass doors, and down a flight of steps. The maze went on.

As they stepped outside, once again, the heat smacked her in the face. Luckily, Sandy had brought her camouflage hat and pink sunglasses, which she quickly slipped on.

They walked through the tire, tractor, and detail shops. There was even a dog park and wash. These people had thought of everything. They walked past loaded and empty trailer lots. A Frisbee golf course lined the perimeter. There was a pavilion with several semis parked in front of it, and several drivers were lounging around at tables. A training pad covered several acres. They walked past the truck wash and saw a massive inbound terminal and training facility. As usual, Sandy was drenched in sweat and the last person in her group to make it to the plaza building, which was the last building on their tour.

Her ex-husband had once told her kids, "You know your mom moves like fucking pond water." She, however, likened her movements to her spirit animal, the sloth. She was slow and steady, but she always finished the race.

Okay, maybe that was a turtle. But in the end, whether she was sweaty or not or as slow as a sloth or a turtle, Sandy made it inside.

Jamie finished the tour with the inbound-outbound section, where all incoming and outgoing semis arrived and left from, and all departments and classrooms on the floor below them were located. The real world of trucking had begun. Several trainers were on the training pad with their tractors, and Sandy and the rest of the students went out to meet with them. She was happy to see that some of the other students who hadn't been cleared that morning had also come.

Trucks were lined up, hoods were open, and trainers were ready for students and their questions. Some had their trucks ready for students to drive around the test pad. Sandy made a beeline for a beautiful green Freightliner. Two other students climbed in. The inside of the truck's cab was neat, tidy, and more spacious than she had thought it would be. This driver kept the lower bunk neat and organized. A Green Bay Packers' comforter was on his bed. *He obviously isn't from Missouri*, Sandy mused.

The trainer introduced himself to the new students. He didn't waste any time showing them how to operate the tractor. When it was her turn to get behind the wheel, the moment felt magical. It was almost like a scene from a movie. As the rays of light came down from the heavens, the voice of God or God sounding like Morgan Freeman boomed out, *And on the eighth day, God created the trucker, female trucker, that is.* Sandy looked around to see if she was the only who had heard the Big Man himself. She must have been because the students were sitting on the bed, and the trainer was in the passenger seat looking at her and waiting. She blinked, shook her head, apologized, and waited for the trainer to give her instructions.

CHAPTER 9

THE WAIT

Friday afternoon, they were dismissed, and several guys in the group were ready to leave with their new trainers. Everyone who didn't get a call from a trainer was to report to class the next morning at 7:00 a.m. She had noticed that all of the women in the class were still hanging around. No women trainers were on the pad today.

Friday night, they received a much-needed break. Sandy spent most of the night on the phone, catching up with her family and close friends. Everyone was excited for her and her adventure. They wished her luck, as she hoped to be on the road within the next week with a trainer. Her mom asked if she was coming home that week, and Sandy laughed and said that it would be quite a while before she made it back home. Her oldest son was worried about her and hoped that she was eating right and getting enough sleep. Sandy sarcastically pointed out that she was the parent in the relationship and that she was fine. Overall, everyone was happy for her, and that made Sandy happy.

Saturday morning started like all the others, only this time, she had a badge. A badge meant that she was officially part of the company—well not officially, but she was on her way. She arrived at class and caught a glimpse of Jamie and his glitter britches as he walked between classes.

"Good morning, sir," Sandy said.

"Good morning, yourself," Jamie returned with a smile.

"Are there any women MSD trainers that will be here this week, or are there mostly male trainers?"

"We have several women trainers. Most of them have students now or are in route to Springfield to pick up new students."

"Someone said something about a night school. What's the difference between night school and going out with a trainer?" Sandy asked, knowing Jamie probably heard these same questions every week.

"Night school? No, we don't have a night school. Just be patient, we will place all students with trainers. Some just take longer than others," Jamie said brusquely, as if he wanted to pacify her and get on with his day.

Sandy walked into the classroom, found a seat next to one of the girls at the front of the room, and said, "Hey, I'm Sandy."

"I'm Stacy, the girl replied and fist-bumped her. Stacy looked like she was in her mid-thirties. She had beautiful caramel-colored skin, and she wore a ball cap with a short puff of hair sticking out the back that reminded her of a bunny's tail. She was on the "butchy" side of stocky. She had big brown eyes and an adorable smile.

"Where you from?" Sandy asked.

"New York," Stacy said in a perfect mixed accent of the Bronx, Queens, and maybe a little bit of upstate New York.

"That's my favorite city in the entire world," Sandy gushed. "I'm from Georgia."

"Wow," Stacy replied, "that's where my girlfriend lives."

The class soon started, and by that afternoon, they took the shuttle over to the training pad and the classrooms that were located there. More trainers had shown up, and more students were picked. Sunday, Monday, and Tuesday were the same: more classes, more time on the training pad, more looking at trucks, and more learning pre-trip and the parts of the truck.

By Wednesday, Sandy felt like she was part of a crew—a girl trucker crew. Her new crew consisted of Stacy, Mahala, Alex, and Shrimp.

Stacy, her New York City girl, had beautiful, big, soulful brown eyes that soaked up the world around her. Right away, Sandy knew that Stacy would be one of her best friends.

Mahala was her Bohemian, east-coast friend who had dreadlocks. A gypsy-like air surrounded her. She had a natural essence to her. She exuded such a level of confidence and ease that Sandy couldn't help being drawn to her spirit.

Alex was tall and big boned. She had a temper like no other person that she knew. With her eyes alone, Sandy thought she could strike down any jackass trucker who crossed her path. She was a lot younger than Sandy was, but Sandy could see a lot of herself in Alex. Okay, maybe she didn't have as many sparks in her eyes. But still, she reminded her of herself when she was much younger.

Then there was Mandy. Mandy wasn't a Mandy, but she was a shrimp, short stuff, and little bit. The more days that they were there, the more nicknames that she accrued. Sandy thought that Shrimp was the one that suited her best. Shrimp claimed to be five foot, but Sandy was sure that Shrimp might be adding shoes to that measurement. She was short and feisty, and she had an attitude that matched Sandy's daughter's attitude, tit for tat. Shrimp was just a few years older than Sinclaire, but they could easily pass for sisters. Sandy couldn't wait to tell her daughter about Shrimp the next time she talked to her.

The crew was nose deep in the engine compartment when Jamie, with jeans' pockets and seams glittering and gleaming in the sunlight, approached them. Sandy was the first to notice him. "Well, hello, sir," she said.

He looked stern and almost like he was upset. "Can you meet me in the conference room upstairs at 15:00?" Jamie asked.

"Sure," Sandy said, hoping everything was okay. He then went and spoke to each of the other girls in their crew. After he left, they had an impromptu powwow session. All questions were spoken at once, creating a frantic cacophony.

"What do you think this is about?"

"Do you think something is wrong?"

"Why did he only come talk to us girls?"

Suddenly, it hit Sandy, and she said, "I bet we're getting picked for night school."

"But Jamie said there wasn't a night school," Alex quickly countered.

"Yeah, but I think he just said that so everyone will think there isn't one." The anticipation was building up inside Sandy.

The crew made their way to the building and up to the conference room where Jamie was waiting for them. They all took their seats, and all five looked like they were going to be shipped to boarding school.

Jamie smiled and stroked his beard. "Relax, y'all. No one is in trouble. I brought you in today to talk to each of you." Grinning at the uncomfortable looks that they exchanged, he continued. "We watch the students throughout the week and look for those whom we feel have potential. And I have one question to ask each of you." All five women looked directly at him. "Do the five of you want to join the night program we have here at MARI?"

Sandy met Jamie's eyes, and he answered before she asked. "Yes, there is a night program, and we don't advertise it. That's why I told you the other day that we didn't have one."

He could see relief on their faces and smiles.

Jamie continued, "We pick students who we think are committed, want to learn, will work hard, be able to work with the night instructors, and learn everything from the MSD program. Instead of going out on the road with a trainer, you will stay here in Springfield. The program is a twenty-one-night program, and it ends when you take the Missouri CDL exam and pass. So do you ladies wanna join the night class Sunday night?"

All five girls look at each other, and their eyes met. They all had the same answer. Their response was an overwhelming, "Yes!"

Fist bumps and face-splitting grins were around the table. The next phase of their journey was about to begin. Jamie gave them the schedule and told them the campus would pair up the girls who didn't have a roommate. They would be moved to a more secluded part of the campus so that new students moving about during the day wouldn't affect their sleep, as they would be sleeping during the day. He quickly went over all aspects of the training, wished them luck, and left.

When Glitter Britches left, everyone just sat there and let the news sink in. In two days, they would be starting—make that two nights. Sandy was on her way to fulfilling her dream. The ladies planned to meet at the truck in the campus parking lot that evening at sundown. They wanted to work together on pre-trip items and decide where they would eat dinner.

Sandy called for the blue shuttle and went outside to wait. The heat of the day smacked her square in the face once more, as she stood waiting in the bright afternoon sun. Sweat was already beading on her brow. But Sandy didn't care. She had hoped to be on the road with a MSD trainer by now, but she had been offered another avenue of training. She now had a plan, and that plan was now in motion.

By the time she made it back to the campus, Sandy was exhausted. After standing outside in the heat all day on the training pad and experiencing the excitement of the impromptu meeting, Sandy was exhausted and craving a nap for the first time in ages. She climbed on the shuttle bus and headed back to the campus. Once she reached the lobby, she checked in with Jay at the front desk. He had the key card for her new room.

She said, "I'll be here for a while. I'm going to the night classes."

Jay winked at her and said, "I know kiddo, I'll be seeing you around."

"Kiddo?" Sandy laughed. "We are not that far apart in age."

Jay just laughed and said, "Enjoy the experience kid. I want to get my CDL one day as well."

"And you will," Sandy told him. "It's never too late." *If I can do this*, she thought as she walked back to her room to pack up her stuff, *anyone can do this.*

Sandy was drenched in sweat from head to toe by the time she packed and moved everything from her original room to her new room. She slid her room key in the slot, opened the door, and heard the shower running in the bathroom. Her roommate was already there. She just didn't know who it was yet.

She looked at her phone. It was five o'clock. It was too early to meet the girls for their pre-trip study session. She considered making some phone calls, but her bed was looking really welcoming at that moment. *Maybe just a few minutes for a power nap*, she thought, as she settled into the bed that was closest to the air conditioner. Just a quick nap is all I need ..."

CHAPTER 10

GIRL CREW, ENGAGE!

Sandy was driving. Her windows were down. The fresh spring air was flowing through the window and swirling through her hair. Her hair was styled into glorious brunette waves, and her highlights sparkled like glitter. The oversized frames of her sunglasses shielded her eyes from the sun. She knew that she almost looked like a model as she drove down the road in her shiny new lime-green Freightliner.

It was almost as if she and her seventy-five-foot beast simply glided over the asphalt and down the highway. Cars and trucks whizzed by her. Windows were rolled down, and Sandy could see the glorious faces of happy little boys and girls, with their fists pumping in the air. Those were the moments that she lived for. Sandy grabbed the cord of the air horn and let it rip. She didn't know who enjoyed it more, her or the children.

Trucks coming in the opposite direction shimmered just like hers did. They had their windows down, and they were driven by beautiful women just like her. *This is the life*, Sandy thought, as the mountains seemed to go on forever. They were glorious mountains that rose toward the heavens.

Clouds were swirling in and around their peaks. Truck after truck of women traveled up and down America's commerce parkway.

When she caught a glimpse of herself in the driver's side mirror, she didn't even recognize herself. She swore she looked just like … like … Melissa McCarthy? "Sandy, Sandy, Sandy, Sandy!"

Suddenly, Sandy was wide-awake. Shrimp was standing over her with her hair wrapped in a towel and a goofy grin on her face. "Girl, what in the world was you dreaming of?" Shrimp asked.

Sandy blinked for a moment as she tried to get her bearings. She realized that she had just woken up to find her new roommate standing over her. Her dream had been so real and lifelike. Soon that would be her out on the road, making it happen, even if she didn't look as pretty as Melissa McCarthy did. *At least, not for the moment*, she thought.

Sandy smiled and crawled out of bed. She splashed water on her face, and then she and Shrimp walked outside to meet the rest of the gang. The sun was still low in the sky, and thankfully, the heat of the day had somewhat subsided. With pre-trip papers in hand and pristine neon-yellow safety vests on, the gang just reeked of rookie newbies. They didn't care. They were a team, gang, club, and girl pack.

Sandy instantly felt the need to capture those moments in a picture and make notes. She jotted down a note to remind herself to buy a journal the next time she went to the store. Then she turned around, told everyone to smile, and captured the moment in a group selfie.

Now it was time to get down to business. Even though the sun had set earlier, Sandy was drenched in sweat. Her hair felt matted to her skull, and her clothes stuck to her skin. The gang had gone over the truck, trailer, and each of the different sections with a fine-tooth comb. Several seasoned drivers stopped by to offer assistance while they were trying to identify specific parts of the engine and components of the trailer. They gave helpful tips on remembering the terms.

Sandy was familiar with basic truck and car engine parts, but it was still overwhelming. Having to learn the parts of a much larger engine on a semi, their trailers, and the way to test the air brakes properly was a lot to remember. *There's a lot to learn before we even get to start driving the truck*, Sandy thought.

After a few hours, the girls decided to take a break and walked to the little restaurant down the street from the campus. Music was playing, and the place was packed. Judging by the look of the crowd, more than half of the customers were MARI students or drivers. Sandy felt right at home, even though she knew that she looked like a hot mess. The girls had taken their vests and badges off, stashed everything in their backpacks, and blended in with the crowd.

"Eastbound and down, load 'em up and truckin! We're gonna do what they say can't be done!" Sandy belted out. The whole crew busted out laughing. "You know, that song could have been written about our crew." Crew members nodded their heads in complete agreement.

The waiter came and took their drink order, and the girls finally began to relax and let the activities of the past week roll off their backs. It was Friday night, and the beginning of night school would be there before they knew it. But tonight was just about them and the bond that they had.

"We've got a long way to go and a short time to get there! I'm eastbound. Just watch ol' bandit run!" Sandy and Stacy belted out the last two verses in unison and the crew cracked up.

Shrimp and Alex didn't seem nearly as enthusiastic about old trucker lyrics as the older ladies of the group did.

"It must be a generational thing," Sandy mused.

Mahala had a serene smile on her face as she sat there sipping her lemonade. "Can you believe that in just twenty-one days, we will be getting our CDLs? We need to make a pact right now, that no matter what happens and no matter where we go, we will always stay in touch with each other. Deal?"

All five women put their right fist into the center of the table for one big fist bump.

"Deal!" they said in unison. They spent the rest of the evening eating a fantastic meal, laughing, and enjoying the camaraderie. Sandy realized very quickly that she wasn't as young as she used to be. Shrimp and Alex talked nonstop about boyfriends, parties, and clothes.

Oh My God, Sandy thought. *Was I ever that energetic in my life?* She leaned over and whispered to Stacy, "These young' uns are gonna be the death of me. All I want to do is finish this meal, crawl back to the campus, and find my pillow."

"Girl, I'm with you on that one! But you gotta remember being that young and wild," Stacy said.

Sandy mentally looked back, and she still couldn't visualize such a time. Maybe this was her time. *Because it's never too late, right?* she thought.

Mahala, with her same peaceful energy, laughed softly. "I love all the different energies at this table. That's what makes it so special. It's as if we were handpicked to lift each other up." She sounded so old and wise yet looked so young and un-weathered.

They wrapped up dinner and sauntered back toward the campus. Sandy and Stacy had nothing but sleep on their minds. Mahala planned on washing clothes, and only the good Lord knew where Alex and Shrimp would end up that evening.

Sandy tried not to mother the young ones. She had raised her children. These girls did not ask for her opinion, so she was not going to give it. This was her crew and family. She definitely wasn't their mother, but she was the old lady of the group.

When Sandy finally made it to her room, she took a quick shower, dove into bed, and fell asleep in no time. It had been quite a week. She was exhausted but so proud of where she was. She was so looking forward to starting night school that Sunday.

CHAPTER 11

NIGHT SCHOOL

The shortest weekend on record wrapped up. It was Sunday night, and Sandy was sitting in the third row of the lower classroom at the plaza building. The class was packed. She thought her crew was an eclectic mix of personalities, but the wildly varying personalities in front of her was almost overwhelming.

There were at least twenty women of different ages and ethnic backgrounds sitting in the first four rows of the training room. Surprisingly, a couple of men were in the class as well. The whole scene reminded Sandy of watching behind the scenes of a hit TV series, as all the actors waited to play their parts. Sandy had quickly found a seat, removed her new journal from her backpack, and begun to make quick notes on the new characters.

Earlier in the week, not only had Sandy dreamed of driving and being on the road but also dreamed of her new life, as crazy as it was to be starting over at forty-five years old. Her life finally had meaning. She planned on documenting everything that she could. *Shouldn't it include notes, stories, and pictures?* Sandy wondered. She didn't want to forget a thing. She wanted to share her journey. With whom, she wasn't quite sure yet. But somewhere along this journey, she would figure it out. It was twenty-five minutes before the instructors arrived, and Sandy had already jotted down a couple pages of notes on some very savory characters.

Sandy and her kids had a ferocious need to compare people to movie characters and to quote obscure and inappropriate movie lines, so a lot of her notes consisted of movie character's names, habits, quirks, and nicknames, in lieu of actual names.

Lizta, the Mexican seductress, who was outfitted in combat boots and a low cut shirt and had a spiky hairdo, scanned the room. She looked friendly and comfortable, but her spiked hair gave her a bit of an edgy look.

GG was young and fresh-faced. She had the most adorable dark freckles all over her nose and cheeks. She sat bundled up in a heavy jacket, as if it were winter. Sandy decided that she would call her Freckles.

Sherry, an older blond with dark roots and dark circles under her eyes to match, was holding court in the front row. Her high-pitched voice was already making Sandy's eye twitch. Sandy made eye contact with Alex and immediately knew that they were thinking the same thing: *Know what all!* Alex rolled her eyes, and Sandy bit back a giggle.

Amy was tall and thin and acted as if she didn't belong in such a class. She sat alone, reading a novel and oblivious to all other activity in the room. Sandy didn't get one good vibe from her corner of the room.

Jennifer could've been straight off of the set of *Friends*. She had fantastic hair, eyes, and eyelashes. The few guys who were in the class definitely had their eyes on her. She had a classic girl-next-door look, but she was drop-dead gorgeous at the same time. You couldn't help but smile when she looked in your direction.

Patricia looked like she was ready to hike the Appalachian Trail at the drop of a hat. She wore hiking boots, mom shorts, and a floppy fishing hat. She had her hair styled in two braids like a teenager, but she looked like she could hike forty miles further than any teenager in today's world. She had weathered skin and wrinkles around her eyes. She immediately came across as an old soul.

Erica had a bright African-print head wrap, which was twisted high on her head. Her black T-shirt and shorts looked almost dull compared to her lively head wrap. She had a contagious laugh, which sounded low, rumbling, and as if it came from deep within.

Sandy was in the middle of jotting down notes about another girl on the other side of the room, when the doors opened and four night instructors walked in. Sandy was shocked at what she saw. She hadn't known what to expect when coming into class that night, but she was definitely surprised when the door opened.

Daphanie had a bright wild curly red mane, which framed her tiny face. She wore bright-red glasses that matched her hair. She was short and cute, and she had freckles as far as the eye could see. She wore a faded rock-band T-shirt and a pair of men's basketball shorts. Sandy liked her aura immediately. She led the others to the front of the class. Red was the perfect nickname for her.

Rami was close behind Daphanie. He was tall, dark, and handsome, in a villain of a Blockbuster movie sort of way. He spoke with a thick accent. *Maybe French? Armenian?* Sandy couldn't decipher it at that moment. He wore a black T-shirt, shorts, and solid-black baseball cap. *Charismatic* and *charming* were the first two words that came to Sandy's mind and she smiled. The man just oozed a laid-back, self-confident air about himself.

Sandy caught a glimpse of Mahala out of the corner her eye and whispered out the corner of her mouth, "I see you like the bad-boy type." Mahala jabbed her index finger between Sandy's sixth and seventh ribs. Sandy had to fight back a giggle. Sandy whispered out of the other side of her mouth to Stacy, "I guess we know who is off limits to us!" and both girls snickered.

Stacy quipped, "Yeah, well, he's not my type."

Sandy whispered, "What guy in here is?" only to have Stacy jab her index finger between Sandy's fifth and sixth ribs on her left side. "Ouch!" Sandy murmured, rubbed both sides of her ribs, and smiled.

Ralph followed Rami. He was middle-aged and graying at the temples. He sported a camouflage hat with some NASCAR driver's number and name on it and a matching T-shirt to boot. Loud, shifty-eyed, and squirrely, the man just reeked of cockiness. He was talking quite animatedly to the guy behind him. The nickname Professor Dickweed instantly came to mind.

The last instructor was Owen. Owen was listening to Ralph, but is expression said that he could care less about what was being said. Professor Dickweed was so oblivious that he continued to tell his story.

Owen definitely had a military background. They could see it in his walk and posture. He was the only instructor wearing some semblance of a uniform. He wore a pullover that said, "MARI TRUCKING," and khaki shorts. He had several lanyards around his neck. Bald with a shockingly white goatee, he was a ruggedly handsome man. He was quiet and stone-faced while he scanned the room as if he was looking for a suspect. He was definitely not like the other three instructors. He looked like he was all about business.

Red immediately started roll call, and the class quickly quieted down. Everyone was accounted for. Sandy, Alex, Stacy, Mahala, and Mandy were the new students of the week.

Sandy and Stacy were assigned to Owen, and they quickly bumped shoulders to celebrate. Alex and Mandy were assigned to Ralph. Sandy knew that was a great choice for them, but she wasn't sure if it was for Ralph. Little did he know what was coming his way.

Mahala was assigned to Rami's team. "Bow chica bow wow w w w w w w w," Sandy sang under her breath, only to have Mahala jab her entire fist into Sandy's rib cage. *Geez, I am gonna have to toughen up if I am gonna take any more shots to the body*, she thought and giggled.

The instructors discussed the rules and expectations for classroom and training-pad conduct. A basic itinerary for the entire week was given for them to jot down. Once everyone was on the same page, class was dismissed, and everyone headed outside.

Stacy and Sandy quickly found the group that Owen taught and began to walk out to his training pad. Sandy was happy to see that GG and Litza were part of this group, as well as two other ladies named Martha and Peg.

Peg was from Chicago. She told Sandy and Stacy that she already held a class B CDL and that she just needed a refresher course. She was expecting to test out at the end of the week. She informed them that she would be high priority.

High priority meant students who already held a Class B CDL, and they were the first to teach and test. Most of the time, it didn't take too long for these students to get through the program.

She quickly gave Sandy and Stacy the 411 on what to expect. Pre-trip review would take place with Red every other night. They would drive and learn to back up the truck with Owen on the other nights. She told them,

"The faster we learn, the faster we get on the road." That was exactly what Sandy wanted to hear.

Owen came out to the training pad, introduced himself to Sandy and Stacy, and informed them that they would be working with Red that night. Stacy, Sandy, and GG formed a mini-group and walked back over to the plaza building to speak with Red.

Red was a brilliant instructor. With clipboard in hand, she quickly went through the list of sections and verbiage that she wanted them to learn. She moved quickly and with ease. They went from one end of the tractor to the undercarriage of the trailer and back around. Several students at a time went inside the cab of the truck, as she showed them the proper way to conduct an air-brake test. Sandy scribbled notes in the margin of her papers. There was a lot to learn.

The sun was still out, and the heat was still lingering, so of course, Sandy was sweating like a pig. Before she knew it, it was time for lunch. She and Stacy walked inside for some ice water and made their way to the shuttle that was going to the café. Sandy's T-shirt and shorts clung to her, and her hair was matted to her head. She was hot and a little bit overwhelmed, but she was still smiling.

"Roll on, big momma. They gonna do what they say can't be done," she sang and laughed.

"You and your songs," Stacy said and laughed.

"You'd better get used to it," Sandy said as she winked. "We've got a long way to go and a short time to get there."

Stacy helped her finish. "We're eastbound. Watch ol' bandit run!" Several of the other girls looked at Sandy and Stacy like they were nuts. Maybe they were nuts, but Sandy hadn't been this happy in years. Night class resumed.

Sandy was drenched and exhausted by the time the shuttle took them back to the campus. She felt like she was in college again but without the partying. All she wanted was a cold shower and her bed. Shrimp was already in the room changing her clothes by the time Sandy opened the door.

"Alex and I are gonna walk to the store. You wanna go?"

"I have enough energy to take a shower," Sandy said and wished that she had half the energy that Shrimp and Alex had. A cold shower was just what Sandy needed, and the heat of the night quickly washed down the drain. She was in bed and sound asleep by the time Shrimp made it back to the room an hour later.

Sandy was surprised at how well she had slept for the better part of her night. She woke up to her wild head of hair, which she quickly threw into a messy bun. She brushed her teeth, washed the sleep out of her eyes, and texted Stacy. To her surprise, Stacy was already outside waiting for her.

"Good morning, sleepy head," Stacy teased. They both went to find some lunch.

"Today's the big day!" Sandy exclaimed. Stacy looked puzzled. "We get to actually drive today," Sandy said while almost jumping up and down. She felt like a little kid.

"Yes we do," Stacy said. They hopped along the sidewalk.

They arrived at the plaza an hour early, and stood outside to watch several trainers with their students. Some of the trainers and students had just come in off the road, and they were working on backing maneuvers. Others were waiting anxiously while their students were being tested by examiners. Examiners wore red-and-white pullovers.

Sandy pulled out her journal and made some quick notes. "Ed, Edd, and Eddy," she jotted down, affectionately nicknaming the red shirts. *Ed, Edd, and Eddy* had been one of her son's favorite Saturday morning cartoons when he had been younger. The red shirts had an office at the back of the training room. Ed and Eddy were lounging about. She could see them through the window while sitting outside.

One of the Eds stepped out of the tractor, which had pulled in from the plaza with a student at the wheel. With clipboard in hand, Ed made his way to the trainer, as the student followed closely behind him. The trainer looked like an expectant father standing outside of the labor-and-delivery room of a hospital. Concern was on the brow of the trainer as Ed pointed to different lines on his clipboard. Suddenly, smiles brightened all three faces, which were followed by slaps on the back. Then handshakes and hugs commenced.

Sandy knew without a shadow of a doubt that his student had passed his test. She didn't even know the student, yet Sandy was thrilled for him. This was the first time Sandy heard the word *trifecta* and asked its meaning. One of the trainers standing nearby explained, "You have to pass the pre-trip, backing-up portion, and the road test in the first attempt. That's what we call the trifecta. And if the recruiter didn't tell you, you get a $250.00 bonus." He said this with a wink.

Hot diggity dog! Sandy thought. *I wanna be a part of the trifecta club.*

Sandy made her way inside a little too early for class and found her seat. She squeezed in between Stacy and Mahala, with an overly dramatic, "Pardon me, do you have any Grey Poupon?" in her British accent. Alex and Shrimp turned around and looked at her. This old commercial reference was obviously way before their time. "Mustard!" Sandy said and laughed. "It's an old mustard commercial." Neither of the young girls laughed but rolled their eyes. Yep, both of these girls could be her daughters. Their eye rolls were on point, just like Sinclaire's was.

Mahala told Stacy about driving on the previous night with Rami. She looked as if she had a little schoolgirl crush on him. Sandy couldn't wait to drive that night. Stacy felt the same way.

CHAPTER 12

THE RUSH

Starting the truck by herself, Sandy felt a rush. Owen was standing next to the driver's door, and she was alone in the cab. *This feels great*, she thought as she pushed the numbers for the alarm code and started the truck. The truck rumbled to life, and the vibrations of the diesel motor ran through her feet and hands. *This is it*, she though, and concentrated on her instructor's words.

With her foot on the brake pedal, she pushed the yellow knob for the tractor and the red knob for the trailer's brakes on the dash. As the tractor jumped to life, she pressed down hard on the brake. Slowly, she moved her foot to the accelerator, and the truck began to move.

Her goal was to drive to the end of the training pad, stop, and back up straight. That didn't exactly happen. She did well moving forward, but the backing up was a different animal. Owen was a patient instructor. He held onto the driver's side mirror the entire time and instructed her on how to move. Before she knew it, her allotted time was over, and it was Stacy's turn in the drivers' seat.

Sandy felt defeated. It was so much harder than she thought it was going to be.

GG grinned, seemed to read her mind, and said, "That was harder than you thought it was going to be, wasn't it?"

"Oh, my goodness, yes!" Sandy exclaimed. "I think I bombed it."

"Bombed it?" GG said. "Oh no, girl, you did just fine. You'll get another turn in a minute. It gets easier every time you get a chance."

Sandy watched as Stacy drove forward and backed up, over and over again. Then it was GG's turn. GG jumped in like a seasoned pro, perfected a couple of straight line backs, and then moved on to some offset maneuvers. GG told her that she had been in class for two weeks before she and Stacy had arrived. Sandy could definitely tell.

Sandy got back in the driver's seat. Her heart was racing as she pulled forward. Owen, strong and steady, was as patient as they came. Making the most of her time, she repeatedly tried on the training pad. Every time she turned the key, it seemed as if the time flew by. Her time in the driver's seat was up before she knew it. She wanted to stay in the driver's seat all night but knew that she was one of three students.

The class took the shuttle to the Millennium for dinner. Mahala asked Sandy how training was going.

"I'm new. I don't know what to do," Sandy quipped, quoting from the movie *Joe Dirt*, one of her favorite movies. *All I need is a mullet and a ratty mustache*, she thought. "I can't wait to do the drive in town tonight," Sandy told Mahala.

"I went last night, and it was incredible," Mahala said.

"I'm sure it was," Sandy said, winked, and nudged Stacy in the shoulder.

"Knock it off, you two!" Mahala said, but her eyes said something different.

"We see the way you look at your instructor," Sandy said and laughed. Mahala just smiled. Stacy laughed and danced a jig.

Sandy knew that climbing into the truck for her first drive would be etched in her memory forever. Owen went through a basic rundown of what to expect for their first drive. Sandy and GG sat in the back of the cab on the bunk, and Stephanie sat up front in the passenger seat.

He drove them to an industrial park and showed them the way to perform a proper emergency stop. The next few minutes felt like an adult version of a Chinese fire drill, as seats were swapped and the students got to drive for the first time. Owen instructed them on logging into the Qualcomm before driving. All drivers had to log in as the active driver before driving. They had to log out when their drive was complete so that no one else would drive on their clocks. There was so much to learn about trucking.

When it was Sandy's turn to drive, she was alert and nervous. Just as on training pad, Owen was steady and calm. He instructed them from the passenger's seat with a firm hand and steady voice. *This man knows how to teach*, Sandy thought. Sandy soaked up the knowledge like a sponge.

She drove through town and turned wide at the corners. She watched her trailer and all seven mirrors, looking to the right and to the left. She drove about thirty miles. By the time she stopped in front of the plaza, she was spent physically and mentally. She had made it through her first drive. This was definitely something that she would write about that night in her journal, when she returned to campus tonight.

By the time the shuttle took them back to the campus, all crew members were exhausted. Sandy was actually surprised to see Alex and Shrimp being as quiet as the rest of the gang. Rami was driving the shuttle, and the music was blaring. It felt more like a party bus instead of the company shuttle.

Sandy sat back and smiled, as she thought of the night that she had just had and the memories that she wanted to capture before her bed called her name. Several students sang along to the song that was playing on the radio. Sandy put her head on Stacy's shoulder and enjoyed the ride to campus.

The next several nights played out in the same fashion. Pre-trip was almost memorized to perfection, part by tractor part. Sandy and Stacy made a great dynamic duo and worked together like peanut butter and jelly. The drives through town were going great, and Sandy felt very confident in her abilities.

The backing maneuvers, however, were much harder to excel at. Try as she might, Sandy couldn't back up her trailer in a straight line to save her life. She couldn't figure it out. Owen told her to turn right to move left and vice versa. Still, moving the steering wheel didn't seem to be working for her. She was getting frustrated, but her instructor remained patient and talked her every time she messed up.

Through every wrong turn of the steering wheel, he was there with his green laser pointer in hand, calmly instructing. She told Owen that he was a great instructor. He was a quiet a man. Some might have even called him an introvert. Sandy thought he was awesome. But she noticed that he didn't exactly take compliments too well. The color of his cheeks changed several levels of red when she did compliment his training style.

Sandy's time was up, so she turned off the truck, climbed down, fist-bumped Owen, and moonwalked past Stacy and GG. Both giggled. GG climbed into the truck.

On their walk to the plaza for a quick break, Sandy told Stacy a joke. "What did one lesbian frog say to the other lesbian frog?"

"I dunno."

"We really do taste like chicken."

Stacy fell over with laughter, as Sandy doubled over at the waist, laughing at her own joke.

"What's so funny?" Red asked as she walked by.

Still laughing, Stacy said, "Sandy and her jokes."

Red looked at Sandy quizzically. Sandy repeated the joke. Red dragged Sandy over to Rami, Ralph, and several students who were milling around behind Ralph's pickup. "You guys need to hear this."

All eyes were on Sandy as she repeated the joke, laughing while she told it again. The entire group burst into laughter. Sandy continued, "What do you call a broke white person?" There were quizzical looks around her. "Cracka lackin'!" There was more laughter.

People were still laughing when Owen walked toward the plaza building. Red called him over to the group. "Hey, Sandy, tell Owen the frog joke." Sandy repeated the joke for the fourth time. Everyone's eyes were on Owen's face. His face turned bright red. He smiled, shook his head, and walked into the plaza. The ladies went back their groups. The heat of the night clung to their skin.

Every night, especially when they worked on pre-trip, Sandy stepped into a new role that surprised and made her quite popular: stand-up comedian.

"What's the only sound you hear when a water truck hits a vinegar truck head-on?" Sandy asked no one in particular. "Douche!" she yelled, with her hands in front of her like she was sliding into home base.

Sandy forgot just how funny she actually was until she came to trucking school. She used to be so funny and light-hearted. She had loved making everyone laugh. Then life happened, and she lost her light, laughter, and soul. Now that light was back, and so was her passion for life. She laughed every night, as she worked on her new career. Salty and a little bit raunchy and more than off colored, but laughter was shared among friends. No one was offended, but everyone enjoyed a good laugh among friends.

In the midst of every comedy hour, the group had to tolerate Sherry. Sherry was, beyond a doubt, the most annoying, know-it-all; however, she "didn't know her ass from a hole in the ground," as Alex had so nonchalantly stated more than a time or two. Sandy completely agreed with her accurate assessment. She was belligerent, rude, manic, and a downright asshole. This particular night, she was running her mouth about her knowledge of pre-trip, yet she couldn't tell Red what a third of the parts of the tractor and trailer were. When Red that said she needed to study more, Sherry threw a fit like a teenager and claimed that she knew more than anyone on the training pad.

To up the ante, she went so far as to claim that she could out-back and outdrive Rami, Ralph, *and* Owen. Those within earshot knew that Sherry wouldn't last. At some point, she would push someone's wrong buttons and be sent home. She had come into the program three weeks before Sandy and her crew had, but based on her performance, no one could tell.

"What's long, hard, and full of seamen?" Sandy asked, laughing. "A submarine!" There were belly laughs from everyone in the crowd, except Ralph. Apparently, former sailors didn't think that was a funny joke.

Sandy was still laughing as she walked back out to the training pad. GG was working on parallel backing maneuvers, and then it would be Sandy's turn.

***

Night school was flying by. Sandy loved driving late at night. She felt like she was doing a great job of driving through town and on the interstate. She was doing well with pre-trip. She knew all the parts of the tractor and trailer, and she was working on making sure all of her verbiage was correct. Her backing skills were coming along nicely.

Finally one night, it was as if a light bulb had gone off in her head.

Suddenly, the steering wheel was her friend, and little maneuvers made all the difference in the world.

Several days later before class started, everything came to a head when Sherry was called to an office located in the back of the classroom. The door was shut, and the instructors and their boss was inside.

Sandy's nosiness got the best of her, and she suddenly needed some hand sanitizer. She quickly walked to the back of the room and near the office door. She stood at the hand-sanitizer dispenser, which was also located there. She was straining to hear any sound from within. Then she heard, "I knew you were gonna fuck me over!" Sherry screamed.

That was enough hand-sanitizer time for Sandy. She quickly found her seat as a couple of security guards entered the classroom from the lobby and knocked on the office door in the back. Sherry's time with the class had come to an end. She was escorted out of the building, swearing like a sailor the entire way. No one in the class said a word, but a huge sense of relief was felt by all.

The instructors eventually came out, and roll call got everyone back on track. The girls gossiped like old biddies all night long. Sherry sure made her mark on the place.

They spent several nights inside the classroom. Heavy storms rolled through nightly, and the lightening made it unsafe to be on the training pad. They played a homemade game of *Family Feud* with pre-trip sections. The best night of confinement was spent watching *Smokey and the Bandit*.

Daphanie drove to a nearby convenience store and stocked up on bags of cheesy popcorn for the entire class. It was storming like crazy outside, but inside, vintage Burt Reynolds, Jerry Reed, and Sally Field reigned supreme. The night was awesome.

Classes had finally got back on track, and the heat of the night still had Sandy at a disadvantage. As usual, she was standing on the training pad, sweating like a pig. GG was performing her last parallel maneuver. Owen was there with stopwatch in hand and a whistle perched between his lips in case of a safety cone or line encroachment. GG was almost ready to test. Sandy was getting excited for her. She wasn't too far behind her. *A couple more weeks*, she thought.

"Sandy," Owen said as he motioned with his green laser pointer. "You're up."

TEST DAY

It was test day. They had been through six long weeks of night class, and the day was finally here. So many students were in class that the original twenty-one-day program took somewhat longer. Each instructor had too many students at one time to meet the twenty-one-day program. It didn't matter because it was test day.

Mahala passed and trifectaed on Wednesday. Today was Sandy and Stacy's day. They boarded the shuttle at 6:00 a.m. and sat in the second row of the downstairs training room. Ed, Edd, Eddy, and maybe their brother Darryl sat in the front row facing all the students and their trainers. Sandy thought her nicknames for the examiners fit them to a tee.

The last few nights had been a whirlwind of evaluations, mock road tests, sweat, tears, prayers, and backing maneuvers. She was ready though, and so was Stacy.

Owen had a rule that all students had the night off before test day. Sandy spent the better part of the day sleeping and the other part alone. Meditation was never her thing, but Sandy spent most of Thursday afternoon walking and soaking in the beauty of a local park. She needed that very much. Her mind needed the release. She walked and tried not to think of anything that pertained to Friday's exam. She was ready for it. She had been born ready. Tomorrow, she would prove it to herself, her family, and the world.

Juice, one of the red shirts, brought Sandy's brain back into focus by turning on the overhead projector. A list of all the students testing that day came into focus. Stacy was number three on training pad four, and Sandy was number three on training pad two. The butterflies within her were suddenly on high alert.

Juice would be Sandy's examiner. She was stoked. Out of all the Ed, Edd, and Eddys, he was by far her favorite. Juice was tall and aged to perfection. He had hair that was peppered with gray, a constant three-day-old beard, and a voice as smooth and warm as the best-aged brandy. He had a cockeyed grin that matched the mischievous glint in his eye. He nicknamed Sandy Trouble, the first day he met her, and she liked that. *Me trouble? Nah, not me,* she thought. But it made her smile every time she saw him.

Once all the students were registered, the oldest Ed said, "We have a long list of students testing today, so we want you guys to get out there and drive. Drive it like you stole, if you know what I mean." He smiled and winked, and the entire group stood up and moved outside.

Once the student was on the test pad with the examiner, their trainer had to be inside. "I guess they don't want any hand signals between trainer and trainee to occur," one of the trainers said when Sandy asked. Luckily for Stacy and Sandy, none of the night instructors was on-site for test day. But they had each other. Both of them were nervous, but it was in a good way. They sat on the steps and watched the first two students on the training pads.

Time seemed to move in slow motion. The first student on training pad four finished first, and he looked like he had passed. His smile stretched from one side of his face to the other. It was contagious. It made Sandy and Stacy smile just watching him walk toward his nervous trainer, who had just walked out of the plaza to meet him and the examiner. Bear hugs and handshakes confirmed what the girls thought.

The student on pad two finished next and looked just as happy. He walked toward his trainer with his red shirt in tow. Sandy and Stacy stood up. They would both be up after the next student. They walked toward the building, as butterflies mated and morphed within Sandy.

Thirty minutes later, Juice pulled the tractor and trailer from pad two and parked it in front of the plaza building. The student was in the passenger's seat, and he did not look happy. Someone behind Sandy and Stacy told them that the student had failed the backing maneuver portion of the test.

"How can you tell?" Sandy asks him.

"The examiner has to drive the truck to the plaza. The student isn't allowed to drive once they fail."

Sandy's eyes met those of the student, and she smiled sweetly and patted his shoulder. "You'll get it next time!" The student half-heartedly smiled back.

Sandy looked at Stacy, and suddenly, the butterflies became monsters in her stomach. "Oh my God, girl, I'm next."

Stacy grabbed her hands and said, "We both are going to trifecta. I just know it! Good luck, Sandy. You are going to rock this."

"Good luck when it's your turn," Sandy said to Stacy, and they hugged tightly.

Sandy nervously paced until Juice came back outside. He asked which truck she was going to use for her test. She pointed to the gray lightweight Freightliner that they had used for class every night. Juice walked toward the tractor and trailer, and Sandy walked toward training pad two.

Juice parked the tractor in the center of the training pad and walked over to Sandy. "Nervous?" he asked with a crooked grin.

"Yes and no," Sandy said.

"Well, I know you're gonna knock it out of the park, kid. There are a couple of highway patrol officers walking around. They are here to monitor and evaluate us as examiners, not you. So don't let them intimidate you, okay?"

"Sure. Why would a state trooper watching every turn of my truck make me nervous?" Sandy croaked, suddenly nervous to the umpteenth degree. Her palms were suddenly clammy, and a bead of sweat rolled down the back of her neck and into the neckline of her shirt.

Juice, with hi sexy voice, brought her back to reality. "Okay, ma'am, for the pre-trip portion of the test, you have to describe the coupling section, the trailer, and the in-cab inspection. Sandy was stoked. She knew these sections thoroughly.

She walked over to the place where the tractor and trailer joined. Then she started her spiel. "These air hoses are connected at both ends," she said, pointing to the place where the air hose connected to the tractor and the glad hands connected to the trailer. "Both hoses have no abrasions, bulges, or cuts." Her verbiage was on point and Sandy was off to the races.

Sandy and Juice walked along the trailer. Sandy called out each part and touched or pointed as close as she could to the correct part. She was sweating and smiling, and her confidence soared with each step. Juice kept marking the list on his clipboard as they went along. She finished the two outside sections, and they both climbed inside the cab.

Sandy continued her spiel, naming all required parts of the in-cab. She may have pulled on the air horn just a tad too long, but Juice had just smiled, and Sandy had giggled nervously. "I love that sound," she said, sounding like a little girl. She performed the air-brake tests to perfection. She demonstrated that her brake held pressure, and the alarm sounded when too much air was pumped out. She started up the tractor, jumped out to remove the chocks from the steer tires, and got back in to rev up the engine to build up the air pressure that she had just pumped out with the brake pedal.

While they sat inside waiting, they watched as the Missouri State Highway Patrol officer walked toward their training pad.

"I take it, he's coming our way?" Sandy asked, knowing the answer to her own question.

"You know it!" Juice smiled.

Sandy finished the tug and brake tests and told Juice that she was done with the pre-trip portion. He fist-bumped her, and they climbed out to begin the backing-up portion of the test.

One test down and two to go, Sandy thought, as she closed her eyes and said a quick prayer.

With clipboard in hand and whistle on standby, Juice gave her the number of points that were allotted for infractions and the number it took to fail. Sandy could score up to twelve points and still pass the backing-up portion. She hoped to score a zero. The first test was a given. It was to back up in a straight line. Sandy sat in the driver's seat. She closed her eyes and took a deep breath.

"Sandy, you got this," she said out loud to herself. "It all comes down to these maneuvers, and you got this girl!" Mentally pumped, Sandy began the maneuver. She nailed it.

Sandy placed the transmission in park, pulled the brakes, and pulled on the air horn. Juice gave her the thumbs-up, as the state trooper busily made notes on his clipboard.

Juice told her that the next maneuver was the left-side offset. Sandy moved the truck into the proper starting position and closed her eyes again. "Just two more, girl. You got this," she whispered loudly to herself. "You got this," she repeated. Boom! She nailed it. Sandy's emotions were climbing, and she tried to contain herself and remain focused. Again, she placed the tractor in park, pulled the brakes, and pulled the air horn. Juice gave a thumbs-up while the state trooper busily scribbled on his clipboard.

It was the last maneuver. Juice walked over to the tractor, looked up, and told Sandy, "Well, ma'am, I'm going to move the cones, and your final maneuver will be the right-side parallel."

Right-side parallel, Sandy thought, smiled, and tucked her hair behind her ears. This is it.

It was the last maneuver. She had yet to make one mistake or infraction. She had to get to get this one done. She closed her eyes. Tears formed in the corners. She took a long deep breath. She had worked so hard for this moment. She was going to own the moment.

Sandy started the maneuver. She hit all reference points to get her tractor and trailer in between the lines. She backed up and heard Juice blow the whistle. That meant she had backed up too far and gone out of the box. That was two points. But that also meant that all she had to do was pull forward five feet, stop, pull the brakes, and pull the cord for her air horn. She did it.

She had just passed the backing-up section of the exam. She only had the road-test portion left, and she knew that she would nail it. She climbed out of the tractor.

Juice grinned and said, "You ready to drive?"

"You know it!" she almost yelled, elated at her progress.

He had her release her trailer brake so that she could move the tandems when he pulled the release pin. This moved the trailer tires forward to the fourth hole from twelfth hole. She was now ready for the road test.

The passenger door opened. The state trooper climbed in, moved to the back, and sat on the bed while holding the clipboard in his lap. Juice climbed in the jump seat, buckled his seat belt, and said, "All right, student, are you ready to drive?"

Sandy's huge smile could have been her only answer, but she said "Yes!"

Sandy pulled forward, turned on her left turn signal, and pulled out of the training parking lot, being careful to make a wide left turn. Juice gave Sandy directions, and she drove with confidence. She looked in her mirrors, watched for signs, and kept a safe distance from other vehicles. Juice kept making marks on the score sheet. She heard the trooper marking away in the back bunk as well.

"Ma'am, have you ever driven a commercial vehicle before coming to MARI TRUCKING?" the state trooper asked Sandy, surprising her and making her smile.

"No sir, not until I came to MARI."

The road test was over before Sandy knew it. Sandy's smile actually hurt her face, as she pulled back into the training pad's parking lot. She knew without a shadow of a doubt that she had passed. She just didn't know her final score.

She parked her rig in front of the plaza building, set her brakes, logged herself off duty on her Qualcomm, turned off the truck, and all three occupants walked toward the building.

"How do you think you did, kiddo?" Juice asked.

Trying to stay humble, Sandy was still smiling when she said, "I think I passed."

"You knocked it out of the park," Juice confirmed.

"It doesn't get any better than that," the state trooper added.

On the outside, Sandy was walking toward the plaza building and smiling like the cat that ate the canary. But on the inside, Sandy suddenly morphed back into the beautiful Melissa McCarthy figure of her dreams. She was decked out in a bright pink tutu, rainbow-colored tights, a tank top, and an off-the-shoulder sweatshirt that would make Jennifer Beals jealous. Her hair was flowing, and she was spinning around with her arms extended.

"I'm never gonna look back. Whoa, I'm never gonna give it up. No, just don't wake me now." The imaginary Sandy sang the lyrics to American Authors' "Best Day of My Life." Just like a needle scratching an LP vinyl, there was a loud screech in her mind, and she was back to reality.

It felt like her feet barely touched the ground all the way to the plaza building. All the faces in front of her were a blur. She had tunnel vision all the way to the double doors. All her hard work had paid off. She had done it. Her heart was fluttering like a hummingbird's wings.

Sandy walked into the training room, smiling and so damn proud of herself. Now all she had to complete was the paperwork to make her an official holder of a class A CDL for the state of Missouri, and she had to wait for Stacy to finish.

CHAPTER 14

MOTHER TRUCKER!

Friday afternoon was an absolute blur. Sandy stayed in the plaza building and nervously waited for Stacy. Forty minutes later, Stacy parked her rig in front of the plaza building. Her smile was a dead giveaway.

Sandy was waiting with open arms. They hugged like the best friends that they become. They had done it. Three down, and two more of their crew to go. Sandy was sure that Alex and Shrimp would be testing by Sunday.

When all the paperwork was finished, Stacy and Sandy split the fee and ordered an Uber driver to take them to the DMV. They were surprised that the DMV's lobby wasn't very full. It didn't take long for both women to get their numbers called. The temporary paper copy of their CDL licenses felt like a golden ticket in their hands. They felt euphoric but drained, both physically and emotionally. Sandy had felt like this many days in the last two months.

They made it back to campus and went their separate ways to relax, rest, and call all their loved ones to share the fantastic news. They planned on meeting up later and taking the shuttle to the plaza so that they could give everyone the good news.

Sandy made a beeline to her room. She needed to call several people. At the top of her list was her mother.

"Hello?"

"Guess who *trifectaed* this morning, Mom?" Sandy practically shouted. Without waiting for her mom to answer, she blurted out, "This girl!"

"Sandy, I knew you could do it. Ever since you were a little kid, once you set your mind to something, you didn't stop until you got it."

Sandy could hear the pride in her mother's voice. Tears pooled in the corners of Sandy's eyes. "I love you, Mommy Jo. Please tell Dad my great news." They talked for a few more minutes and then said their goodbyes so that Sandy could call her children.

She called her daughter next. Sinclaire was just as happy for her as her mother had been. "Oh my God, Mom. That's fantastic. I'm so proud of you. And I miss you so much."

"I love and miss you too, my sweet girl. I hope I make my kids proud of me."

"Momma, you have no idea."

Sandy's oldest son, James, was just as elated. He let out a whoop. He and Sandy shared a crazy victory dance together. Who cared if it was on speakerphone and they were fifteen hundred miles apart. The dance was in unison and just as crazy on both ends of the phone.

Her last call to Mark, her middle son, warmed her heart. He was her pragmatic, shoot-from-the-hip, no-nonsense kid. She started the conversation the same way that she had with her mom and the other kids.

"Yelloooo?"

"Guess who *trifectaed* today? Yo momma!"

"You bad mother trucker, I told you it was never too late."

Sandy teared up and laughed and the same time. "I love you, son!"

"I love you too, momma."

A light bulb went off, and she said, "That's going to be my handle, son: Mother Trucker. And I owe it all to you!"

Sandy had more calls to make, but her bed won the battle. She turned her phone off and the AC on full blast, and she was out like a light in a matter of minutes. Sandy took a much-needed four-hour nap and then walked to Walmart for some art supplies. She had a thank-you gift that she needed to work on before she went to the plaza tonight with Stacy.

Several hours later, Sandy was ready and waiting for Stacy. Sitting on a bench by the cafeteria, Sandy watched as Stacy walked toward her. Stacy was swaggering. Their eyes met, and Stacy's swagger became more exaggerated. By the time she got within ten feet of Sandy, Stacy was moonwalking.

Stacy sat next to her friend, and they compared notes on all the phone calls they had made that afternoon while waiting for the evening shuttle. They felt weird not being part of a group of girls taking the shuttle to class. They had officially *graduated,* and they were now waiting on calls from TNT trainers so that they could start their thirty thousand miles of over-the-road training. They were now official employees of MARI TRUCKING.

By the time the dynamic duo stepped off the shuttle, Sandy had informed Stacy of her new handle, Mother Trucker, compliments of Mark. Her swagger matched Stacy's, as they walked down the steps toward the training pads.

Their first stop was the pre-trip section. They made a beeline toward Daphanie. Hugs ensued, and fist bumps were given all around. Red looked like a proud mother hen, which had two more chicks that were ready to leave the nest.

Mahala was there too. She was going to leave in the morning with her new TNT trainer.

Sandy and Stacy shared their moment with Mahala, along with a new round of hugs. Together they went to find Alex and Shrimp. This was possibly the last time that they would all be together in their little group. They needed one last impromptu group meeting.

Alex had seen the threesome before they had seen her, and she was already walking toward them. Shrimp was not far behind. All the women were talking at once. Mahala was leaving the next day. It would be Alex and Shrimp's last night on the training pad. They were going to test out on Sunday, and they would have Saturday night off. Sandy and Stacey were still flying high on their morning successes.

Even though cell phones were not permitted during night class, all the women made sure they had each other's numbers. Sandy took one last group selfie to capture the moment. The next thirty thousand miles were going to be hard, and they would need each other when they were done. Tears and hugs sealed their friendships like glue. Sandy loved her girls, and she couldn't wait for their adventures to begin.

The last person Sandy went to see was Owen. Her now former instructor was doing what he did best. Owen was in his usual spot, shining his green laser pointer's beam on a tractor's back tire. Sandy had nicknamed Owen the Truck Whisperer during the first few weeks of class. He was patient and methodical, and she swore he could teach a blind man to drive a truck.

When Sandy walked toward him with gift bag in hand, Owen caught sight of her. He motioned to his student to continue practicing and walked toward Sandy. Sandy gave him a shy wave and then laughed. She had no idea why she felt suddenly awkward.

"I heard you made it to the Trifecta Club," Owen said and fist-bumped Sandy.

Sandy was grinning again like a goober. She handed her small gift bag to Owen. Owen looked surprised and asked what was in the bag. "I made you something. A mandala stone. For the best night instructor in the world."

"Thank you Sandy," Owen said with sincerity. "It was an honor to have you on my team." They shared a heartfelt hug. Sandy owed her new life to this man. He had taught her skills that she needed, and now she was on her way out of town.

Sandy joined Stacy in front of the plaza building for a quick impromptu comedy session.

"How do you get a nun pregnant?" Sandy said, grinning and knowing that no one was going to answer. "You dress her up like an altar boy."

By the time they were ready to go back to campus, Sandy had made everyone's sides hurt from all the laughter. Sandy and Stacy boarded the shuttle, and Sandy took one last look at the training pad below her. Her work was done here. She was ready for the open road.

PART 2

CHAPTER 15

ALONE

Sandy sat on the curb and felt like crying and laughing at the same time. It was 3:00 a.m. She was at a TravelCenters of America (TA) truck stop in rural Kentucky, and she was alone—like alone alone. She had no cell phone, trainer, or truck. All Sandy could do was laugh nervously.

The night had started out pretty normal. She and Jessie swapped places at around 10:00 p.m. in Ohio. It was Jessie's turn to drive and Sandy's turn to sleep. During their post-trip/pre-trip inspections, Sandy and Jessie found a leaky hub seal on the front, right, steer tire. Jessie said that she wanted to stop on her thirty-minute break and get a mechanic to look at it.

When Sandy woke up several hours later, the truck was not moving, and Jessie was nowhere to be found. She opened the curtains of the sleeper berth to see that the truck was parked close to the mechanic's bay of the truck stop. *We must be waiting to get the hub seal repaired*, Sandy thought, as she pulled her flip-flops out of her bag and slipped her feet into them. She grabbed her lanyard, truck key, company ID, which also served as her ATM card and hopped out of the truck.

She was out of bottled water, and needed to pee so she decided to stop by the ladies' room while the truck was stopped. She was still in her jammies, but hey, it was 3:00 a.m. in the middle of nowhere, so she didn't think twice about her early morning outfit choice. She'd seen crazier attires at literally every truck stop every day that she had been on the road so far. So being outside the truck in her pajamas wasn't the end of the world.

She walked by the mechanic's bay and glanced inside to see if Jessie was inside talking to one of the mechanics. She found no Jessie, so she went inside to go to the restroom and to buy two liters of water. Then she walked back to the truck, only there was no truck. There was just an empty space where the truck had been parked twelve minutes earlier.

Sandy walked toward the mechanic bays, thinking Jessie had received approval to repair the hub and had moved the truck into the bay. She found no MARI TRUCKING truck. She walked behind the bays, checking to see if the truck was in line and waiting to enter the bay. That was a big nope again. She walked to the fuel island and looked for any sign of their tractor and trailer. She found nothing. Then it sank in. Jessie must have thought Sandy was still sleeping in her berth and drove off without her.

Sandy stood there in disbelief. She didn't have her cell phone. It was still plugged into the charger on the bed. Of course, she didn't know Jessie's cell phone number. As a matter of fact, she couldn't think of *anyone's* number at that time of the morning and in the middle of nowhere.

She trudged toward the customer-service desk next to the mechanic's bay and opened the door. She asked the young guy at the desk if Jessie had happened to stop in.

"Oh yeah, she came through here, but I told her it was a six-hour wait to get her truck in the bay," he said, grinning.

Sandy closed her eyes and laughed. "Do you have a phone I can use?" Sandy grinned. "My trainer took off without me." After the kid stopped laughing, he slid the phone toward her. "And can you Google the main number for MARI TRUCKING please?" He laughed again. Sandy couldn't blame him. This was one for the books.

The night operator at MARI connected Sandy to Rex, her night dispatch.

"Good evening, this is Rex!" Rex boomed. He was obviously a seasoned night owl.

"Hey, Rex, this is Sandy, truck number 78589, and I kinda have a little problem."

"Fire away, driver. What's going on?"

"Jessie stopped to get the hub seal on our passenger's side steer tire looked at, so I left the curtain open and went inside to get some water and use the bathroom. But when I came outside, she was gone." Crickets chirped for several seconds until Sandy heard Rex's laughter burst through the phone. "It's not funny," Sandy said, laughing herself. "Okay, maybe it is a little funny. But my phone is in the truck, and I don't know how to contact her," she said, trying to convey the importance of getting Jessie back to the truck stop. Back to her.

Rex was still laughing when he said, "Let's call Jessie on three-way. This is going to be fun." He placed her momentarily on hold as he dialed Jessie's number. He clicked back to Sandy, and they waited for Jessie to answer. As they waited, Rex told her that it happened more times than she realized. This didn't make Sandy feel any better about the situation.

"Hello?" Jessie finally answered on the eighth ring.

"Good evening, Jess. It's Rex," Rex answered.

"Hey, what's up, Rex?" she asked.

"Missing anything, Jess?" he asked, barely holding back his laughter. Both Rex and Sandy could almost visualize Jessie looking behind her to see to the open curtain.

Jessie blurted out, "Ohhhhhhhhh, shit!" All three phone participants burst out in laughter.

"Oh my God, Sandy!" Jessie practically shouted into the phone. "I thought you were sleeping."

"I was, until you stopped, and I woke up and decided to get some water. I thought you were getting the hub seal fixed," Sandy tried to explain.

Jessie said, "I'll be right there," and ended the call abruptly. Sandy handed the phone back to customer-service guy and walked outside to wait for her trainer.

She walked over to the curb by the portable propane tank's cage, sat down on the curb, and waited. *The last two weeks have flown by*, Sandy thought as she opened one of her cold water bottles and took a long swig.

The day after she had shared hugs with her crew on the training pad, she left with her new trainer and heading toward Joplin with her first load.

Jessie was a straight shooter. She was a no-nonsense woman in her thirties, who could shoot someone down with her eyes alone. Sandy had graciously nicknamed her Ol' Stank Eye. She had told Jessie on more than one occasion that she had missed her calling as an army drill sergeant. Jessie worked, drove, and taught hard. She never slept with the curtain closed. Sandy was amazed at her ability to be awake for situations that needed her attention and her still being able to drive her full shift when Sandy was done.

Sandy and Jessie had already passed the ten-thousand-mile mark of her thirty-thousand-mile requirement, and they had only been on the road for two weeks. They drove to Florida, picked up a load of orange juice, and headed to Washington State. They dropped off the orange juice, picked up a load of apples, and headed to New Jersey. From New Jersey, they drove to Vermont for a load of ice cream, and now they were heading toward Las Vegas.

She couldn't believe that she was getting paid to do it. She loved the lifestyle. She loved seeing all the states and landscapes that she had never been to before. She loved the new sunsets, sunrises, desert terrains, mountains, and hills. She loved the countryside and cities that they drove through. She loved the driving.

Jessie was a hard worker, and she expected no less from Sandy. Jessie was a hands-on type of trainer, and she expected Sandy to retain everything the first time that she told her. If Sandy asked a question, and Jessie had given her the answer previously, the stank eye came out in full force. Sandy was left trying to figure out the answer by herself. When her shift was over, Sandy jotted down everything new that she had learned that day. Every day, she learned so many new things. She was eager to learn more.

"Hey, little lady, you need a ride?" a middle-aged, heavyset trucker asked as he pulled up to where Sandy sat waiting for her trainer.

Sandy shouted over the sound of his engine, "No, I'm good. Thanks!" He seemed to be disappointed in her answer but drove on past her and out of the lot.

"You working tonight, baby?" another trucker asked, not even five minutes later.

"Yes," Sandy said automatically and then realized by the look on his face that he wasn't thinking of trucking. *Oh, my God*, she thought as her face suddenly burned bright red. *These drivers must think I'm a lot lizard, a lady of the night, or a recreational reptile.* Her daughter came up with that title, saying that it was a much nicer title than lot lizard. "I'm mean no!" she blurted out, disappointing another trucker. He drove on past her as well.

A female trucker rolled in right behind the overeager lot-lizard hunters, and based on the look she gave Sandy, she was either praying for her soul or hoping that Sandy wasn't looking for her man. From the look on the woman's face, Sandy guessed she had a man, and was on the defense. But this trucker's husband wasn't who Sandy needed. She wanted Jessie. She just wanted to be back in her own truck.

Where is Jessie? Sandy thought. It felt like forever since Jessie had driven off and left her. Sandy didn't even know what time it was because she didn't have her cell phone. She felt so incomplete without it. She got up from the ground, dusted off her bottom, stood behind the propane cage, hidden from eager drivers, and waited as patiently as possible for her wayward trainer.

This moment was definitely going into her trucking journal. She was sure that she would laugh at herself in the morning, but right now, Sandy only wanted Jessie to swing into the parking lot so that she could climb in and go back to bed. Her shift would be starting in a few hours. Sandy didn't think she'd be happy to see the stank eye.

But as she saw Jessie whip into the parking lot and over to she was waiting, all she could do was smile. Stank eye or not, she was very happy to see her trainer. She climbed into the passenger seat, expecting a lecture from Jessie, but all she heard was laughter. Sandy joined her. It had been quite a night. She felt like Kevin McCallister in *Home Alone*, when his mommy came home on Christmas Day.

CHAPTER 16

DRIVE, SLEEP, EAT, SHOWER, AND REPEAT

Sandy couldn't believe how fast her training flew by. Drive, sleep, eat, shower, and repeat. This was her life. Her brain was on overload during her every waking second, and she loved it. If it weren't for her kids, she would have done it years earlier. Now she couldn't wait for her training to end so that she could get her own truck and start trucking Sandy-style.

But right now, Sandy had a death grip on the steering wheel, and she was maneuvering her rig through on I-5's grapevine in California, as she headed toward Los Angeles. It was 3:00 a.m., and the traffic was already thick. She had downed a Red Bull early on in her shift and stopped a few minutes ago at a Pilot truck stop for her newest favorite drink: a caramel macchiato cappuccino. *Who knew truck stop cappuccinos could be so yummy?* She thought. She was in love. She stopped at a Pilot for her break every chance she got.

She learned that most drivers had their preference of truck stops for various reasons. Pilot was Sandy's favorite by far. She loved the cappuccinos but also the clean showers and thick towels.

She had had no idea that most truck stop's amenities were so nice. She had stopped at truck stops for years to get fuel, snacks, and drinks on road trips. She had never known about the hidden places in the back, which were made especially for tired and road-weary drivers just like herself: drivers' lounges, arcades, barbershops, urgent care facilities, and offices for DOT physicals. Sandy had even tried her luck at a few small casinos on a break while passing through Las Vegas. *The key word is tried*, Sandy thought with a giggle.

Sandy blinked and checked both mirrors. The early morning traffic was bumper-to-bumper, and she was maintaining a good following distance to the car in front of her. Ms. Stank Eye was sleeping in the back. Jessie still left the curtain open when Sandy drove, but Sandy knew that she was doing a good job because she rarely heard Jessie yell at her from the sleeper berth. The phrase, "Watch that trailer in the mirror until it's completely straight behind you," would replay in her mind for years to come. Sandy was certain of that.

Sandy topped the mountain. The white headlights snaking up the mountain to her left and the trail of red taillights that she was following down the winding mountain were beautiful like a vivid abstract painting. There was no moon out this morning. Although it was hot, a light fog drifted in and out of the valley. Sandy was at peace. Even the honking and the rude California drivers didn't faze her. All of the hectic commotion and rudeness washed off her back as if she were a duck. Sandy didn't have an ounce of road rage in her body.

Jessie fussed at her more than once. She told her to be more aggressive. "Do not let other driver's run you over," Jessie preached. But Sandy didn't see it as being run over. She was courteous and friendly, and she smiled most of the time.

On rare occasions, Sandy feared using the bathroom on a moving truck. It wasn't an industry secret that men had a much easier time than women in this department. Some of the nastier men left evidence for the whole world to see. Half-full jugs and twenty-ounce Mountain Dew bottles full of urine were left on curbs. They littered the ground at any given truck stop. Some truckers knew no bounds of nastiness.

Jessie's emergency container of choice was a Styrofoam cup that she picked up at every truck stop that they fueled at. On the first day of training, Jessie had promised her that Styrofoam cups, lids, plastic bags, and hand sanitizer would be Sandy's best friends.

In her eyes, the only problem Sandy had was that she was fat. A fat girl trying to pee in a cup inside a moving truck could be a recipe for disaster. Sandy became majorly anxious just thinking of squatting over a cup behind the sleeper berth curtain while Jessie was driving and going everywhere but the cup. Her yoga pants, sweaty legs, and tiny bathroom stall debacle on her first day of orientation were still fresh and vivid in her mind. At no point did Sandy want to get kicked off her trainer's truck because she missed a Styrofoam cup and drenched her trainer's truck floor instead. *No, thank you*, she thought.

One of the few times that Sandy had felt that Jessie yelled at her had been the time she had pulled off the road and onto the shoulder, during a long desolate stretch of interstate somewhere between Utah and Nebraska. It was 3:00 a.m., and the full moon and the stars lit up the western sky. Sandy hadn't passed a rest area or a truck stop in hours, and her bladder was screaming.

She decided to pull onto the road's shoulder for a quick pop and squat. She looked in her mirrors, clicked on her turn signal, pulled onto the shoulder, pulled her air brakes, and turned on her hazard lights. She quickly logged off her Qualcomm, grabbed some napkins, and climbed down and outside to quickly do her business.

She was in the squatting position on the edge of the grass and looking up when she glimpsed more than twenty deer just on the other side of a fence. Every deer was staring at her. The scene was almost magical. Sandy actually laughed because she was embarrassed that a herd of wild deer had caught her in the act of relieving herself. She finished her business, climbed back inside the truck, cleaned her hands with hand sanitizer, and felt the wrath of Ol' Stank Eye behind her.

"You do know that is unsafe, dontcha?" Jessie barked from the sleeper berth.

"I made sure it was a straight way with no curves, and I used my hazards," Sandy said, defending her actions.

"Only do that in emergency situations, okay?" Jessie barked.

"My bladder deemed it an emergency," Sandy meekly replied as she thought of the emergency feeling her bladder had been experiencing just moments earlier.

Sandy looked in her mirrors, checked for oncoming vehicles, pushed in her brakes, turned on her turn signal, and pulled back onto the road. There wasn't another vehicle in site. Hopefully, Ol' Stank Eye would go back to sleep. Sandy didn't like disappointing her trainer.

Sandy definitely had something to write about in the morning when her shift was over. Of course, she wrote about the magical moment with the deer and not the lecture from Jessie.

Two weeks later, Sandy was driving that same lonely corridor, only this time, it was hot and bright outside, and she was driving in the opposite direction. When the magical-deer memory came to mind, a smile spread across her face. When Sandy looked to her left and across both sections of highway at the shabby jagged fence, she burst out in laughter.

That magical moment two weeks earlier with the wild deer turned out to be a herd of domesticated deer on a farm that produced deer urine used for hunting products. Those same magical deer that had been staring at her that night under the bright moon and stars now stood under a huge company sign touting its products.

Sandy could not stop laughing. Life on the road was just too funny. This would make it into her journal at the end of her shift. She couldn't wait to tell Jessie when she woke up for her shift.

Before Sandy had finished orientation, she had been required to watch tons of videos and take tests on what she had learned. One of the videos she watched was on high value loads (HiVal). HiVals were of the utmost importance, and they had several strict steps that she had to follow to a tee per company policies. In the video, the actors were mostly in-house instructors, and several potential situations were reenacted. The video was kind of cheesy, and it had lots of bad acting, but the points were made.

All rules must be followed. All suspicious activity must be reported, and a driver must always remain alert. The guy playing the suspicious character wore a gray hoodie and flannel shirt. He sat in an old red pickup, watched every move the oblivious truck driver made, and moved in for the kill.

Jessie and Sandy received their first team HiVal load a couple of weeks into Sandy's training. Jessie asked Sandy if she remembered the rules from the HiVal video. Sandy told her that she did. Both girls spoke to dispatch and agreed to follow all the rules. They were to pick up their load in Denver and deliver it in Compton, California, two days later. Sandy was as nervous as a cat sitting next to a rocking chair. Jessie laughed at her student and asked the reason that she was suddenly so nervous.

"Because this is my first HiVal load!" Sandy exclaimed.

Jessie shook her head. "It is a big deal, but it's not. All you have to do is follow the rules and make sure you document on the Qualcomm when, where, and how long we stop, and you'll be fine."

Sandy didn't feel fine. Suddenly, every move she made felt different. Jessie, of course, was a pro. To her, it was a normal day in trucking.

They arrived at the shipper and checked in. They were given a dock door to back up to. *Same as all the others*, Sandy thought and hoped her nervousness would soon leave her. Jessie climbed into her bed for a nap while the shipper loaded the trailer, and Sandy sat in the driver's seat waiting for the load to be completed.

Her shift was normal enough, and she enjoyed the grandeur of the mountains west of Denver. She was still quite nervous when she went down the mountains using her Jake Brakes and cruise control, but she was slowly getting the hang of it. Before she had left her house for training, Sandy had watched several videos on YouTube about the dangers of only using service brakes on steep inclines and the disastrous results. Runaway ramps were a last resort, and she definitely did not want to catch her trailer brakes on fire because she was riding them down the mountain.

Cautious as usual, Sandy made it through the mountains of Colorado. She was well into Utah when her shift ended. She documented each rest break on the Qualcomm. She was feeling better about hauling a HiVal load.

Jessie took over later that night. They were scheduled to arrive at the receivers at around 5:00 a.m. Their appointment was 6:30 am, and if traffic was good, they would be well ahead of schedule.

Sandy went to bed, and surprisingly, it didn't take her long to fall asleep. She woke up just as Jessie was exiting the 105, right at the Compton city limits. She quickly dressed, opened the curtain, and sat down in the passenger's seat to put on her shoes. It was still dark on the west coast, but the traffic was already congested.

Jessie made it to the receivers an hour before their appointment. They were the first truck to arrive. The employees hadn't arrived yet, and it felt eerie to be alone in an industrial park. Twenty minutes later, an older red pickup pulled in, directly facing the girl's truck. A man with a black hoodie and an overcoat was inside it. He left his headlights on, and Sandy felt as if she and Jessie were sitting under an interrogation light at the police station. This guy gave her the creeps. Suddenly, she remembered the HiVal safety video and the suspicious character staking out the driver and his HiVal load. Sandy whispered loudly, "Do you think he's up to no good?"

Jessie looked at Sandy as if she had just grown another head. "What are you talking about?"

Sandy whispered again, "Do you think he looks suspicious? We do have a HiVal load."

Jessie burst into laughter and said, "Girl, you've watched one too many *Breaking Bad* episodes."

"No," Sandy said, "I think I watched one too many safety videos during orientation."

About the time that Sandy stopped talking, another old pickup pulled in. The driver got out and unlocked the gate. Then both pickups pulled through the gate and into parking spots. Sandy felt like an idiot. The grumpy-looking hooded man was only an employee and obviously not a morning person.

Jessie and Sandy went to check in. While Jessie was signing the paperwork, Sandy asked the receiver if they had a restroom that she could use. The receiver said that they did but that she would need an escort. He paged a man's name over the intercom, and guess who showed up at the locked door to escort her to the ladies' room: Mr. Grumpy Pants. But Mr. Grumpy Pants didn't look so grumpy and mean in the lights of the warehouse. Sandy decided that hauling HiVals wasn't as intimidating as she had first thought. She was just glad that this was one was done.

CHAPTER 17

OH, SHIT!

Sandy was down to her last two thousand miles of training with Jessie. Her time seemed to have flown by. She thought about her first day, when she had met Jessie, and the first thought she had had when she had thrown her backpack and duffel bag on the top bunk: *Please, sweet baby Jesus, let this bunk hold my fat ass and not kill my trainer.* She never voiced her concerns to her newly assigned trainer, but the first night that they stopped, and she slept on the top bunk, Sandy held her breath for several seconds as she waited for the impending doom.

"Do you like guacamole?" She had visions of John C. Reilly crashing down on Will Ferrell in the bunk-bed disaster scene in the movie *Step Brothers.* It never came to fruition. For that, Sandy was very thankful. These bunks were much stronger than Sandy gave the manufacturers credit for.

Life on the road wasn't for the faint of heart. That was for certain. Sandy learned how to run her work clock and fall asleep as soon as she docked at a shipper. She was nowhere close to mastering that skill, but Jessie was a pro. She told Sandy to get her sleep whenever she could. If they were waiting on a load at a shipper or to get unloaded at a receiver, Jessie was in her bunk, sleeping away. Sandy napped quite often, but she couldn't switch her mind off. She hoped that she would acquire a talent like her trainer had, the sooner, the better.

Another issue that Sandy struggled with on the road was stomach issues. Besides the stock of Red Bull, Monster energy drinks, and sugary cappuccinos she drank to stay awake, Sandy had also acquired a stockpile of Imodium A-D. The diet of a trucker was not the greatest in the world. Sandy had already started planning truck-friendly meals that she could prepare in her own truck once she upgraded.

But until that time came, Sandy ate Imodium A-D like candy. She knew it wasn't the healthiest habit, but she needed to make it through training in the best way that she could. Her biggest fear was having an accident in the truck because she couldn't get to a rest or truck stop in time. Sandy lost count of the times the *Mission Impossible* theme blared in her head, as she rolled into the fuel island or rest stop with just enough time to do an awkward duck walk to the bathroom. This was the worst part of the job for Sandy. She hoped it would get better once she got her own truck and changed her eating habits and schedule.

Jessie was maneuvering through Friday afternoon traffic. They were hoping to get a decent parking spot for the rest of the day in Ontario. Sandy ranked Southern California in the top ten of her favorite areas since she had started trucking. She climbed into the passenger seat while Jessie was driving. The heat of the day, honking, and traffic noises had awakened Sandy several minutes earlier.

She took advantage of the view from the passenger seat. She kept snapping pictures of the mountains and palm trees. She loved the graffiti on the overpasses and on train cars. It was even beautiful on abandoned buildings along the highway. Sandy loved documenting her journey.

So far, she had twenty-eight thousand miles under her wheels, a phone and Facebook page full of photographs, and two journals full of notes and memories. She didn't know what she would do with all of her memories, but she was sure that Melissa McCarthy would make a great trucker driver if her life's journey ever made it to the big screen. She was sure of it. She would just keep documenting as much as she could, until the time came to put it all together.

The traffic moved along slowly as Jessie and Sandy discussed this last coastal run before heading back to Springfield so that Sandy could upgrade to her own truck. She was stoked. *Adrenaline alone will propel me across the nation,* she thought and smiled. Sandy snapped away, carefully capturing everything of this beautiful west-coast state that she could.

Jessie made it to the TA truck stop. It was only 2:00 p.m. and almost at full capacity. She drove through row after row, looking for a spot and finally finding one in the very back row along the fence that bordered I-5. Jessie snaked her trailer back and easily maneuvered between a J. B. Hunt truck and a high curb, where there was a rocky area with some stubby-looking cypress trees, which were twisted and intertwined with each other. Several piles of dog poo littered the area, and Sandy could see the reason why this was a popular area for man and his best friend.

Once Jessie had parked and logged out, both ladies climbed out of the truck to head inside for a much-needed hot shower and meal. Sandy stopped long enough to take a picture of the cypress trees, which she wanted to send to her oldest son. He would be able to tell her what kind of trees they were.

As she continued inside, Jessie strolled ahead of her. The west coast did not have the humidity of the south, and for that, Sandy was quite thankful. But even with no humidity, the long walk from the large truck stop's back row to the building's interior caused Sandy to be drenched in sweat.

As she opened the door, two female drivers were walking out. Mahala almost shouted Sandy's name. "Sandy! Oh my God, girl. It's so great to see you," Mahala exclaimed and hugged a surprised Sandy.

Sandy hugged her back, grinning from ear-to-ear. "Girl, I have missed you so much," Sandy returned.

Mahala introduced Sandy to her trainer. They talked for several minutes, comparing their training and the time they had left to be trained. Due to their tractor breaking down and spending almost a week at a Freightliner dealership, Mahala was now about a thousand miles behind Sandy.

Jessie brought Sandy her shower ticket, and Sandy quickly introduced her to Mahala and her trainer. All four women spoke for several minutes, until Jessie and Sandy's shower numbers were called out over the PA system. There was another round of hugs, and then Sandy and Mahala parted ways. It was so good to see one of her crew.

Sandy walked upstairs to the showers. She was in no rush, as they would not be picking up their produce load until the next afternoon. They had almost twenty-four hours to relax. She took a long hot shower and then a cool one. She enjoyed every minute of it. She didn't even bother drying her hair. The hot California air would either help dry it or her sweat would keep it damp.

Sandy went downstairs to shop for some audio books and ordered her meal from Taco Bell. As she munched on a chalupa and caught up on her phone's emails, she received a text from James.

"Momma, that looks like several weeping blue spruces," the text read. Sandy hadn't even been close. Sandy had known that her son would be able to identify the trees. He was a walking encyclopedia when it came to plants and animals. He had been like that since he was a kid. They texted back and forth several times, and she informed him that she was almost done with training and that she would be upgraded soon. He told her that he was very proud of her. She promised to call him once she had finished training and made it back to Springfield.

Because the training was so intense, Sandy kept her contact with the outside world to a minimum. She wanted to stay as focused as she could. Plus, she was always so mentally and physically tired at the end of her shift that sleep was always the first thing on her mind.

She finished her meal and decided to order something from Pizza Hut to take back to the truck with for her supper, which she would have later that night. *Having the night off is a nice little reprieve*, Sandy thought, considering how hard she and Jessie had been pushing for the last several weeks.

She got back to the truck as the sun was still hanging in the western sky. Traffic was still snarled up behind them on I-5. That would never change. When she climbed into the truck, the curtains to the sleeper berth were already closed. She knew that Jessie had beaten her back to the truck. She was curled up, watching one of her shows on TV. Sandy pulled down the ladder, closed the curtain, climbed up, and settled herself into bed for the evening.

Sandy took a much-needed nap. It was one of those

knock-you-off-your-feet, all-is-black-around-you, and drool-collecting-on-your-pillow naps. Sandy didn't know what woke her up, but her eyes opened. It was pitch-black. Jessie's TV was no longer on. Suddenly, her stomach rumbled violently, and cold sweat broke out on the back of her neck.

Oh, this is not good, Sandy thought, knowing just how far they had parked from the main building at the truck stop. *There is no way that I am going to make it*, she thought. Her mind raced, and her stomach surged again. She realized that Jessie had put the ladder up sometime during Sandy's nap. She was stuck on the top bunk with no way down.

Sandy sat up and rummaged in her bag for some clothes, not even looking at what she pulled out. "Jessie," she yelled, "please pull the ladder down." Jessie sleepily reached above her head and pushed the lever, and the ladder came down. Sandy was nanoseconds behind it. She was down the ladder and out the door so fast that she was sure Jessie was wondering where she was going in such haste.

She panicked. The truck stop felt like seventeen miles away instead of seventeen rows. But she knew that her stomach wouldn't even make it two rows, let alone seventeen. Her face was red with embarrassment as she ran to the back of the trailer and up on the curb. She looked over at the weeping blue spruce trees and saw a little worn path that went between the shrubs. She made a split-second decision and hoped that no one in the world was watching what she was about to do.

She made it to the shrubs, turned around, and lowered her shorts, just when she couldn't hold it any longer. All Sandy could do was squat there, pulling her long T-shirt to her knees and praying that homeless people had not set up an encampment under the weeping blue spruce trees behind her.

She closed her eyes and finished her business. She was mortified at what she had had to do. As an adult, she had never had an accident like this. But she was there, on a Friday evening in southern California and with the snarling, standstill traffic of I-5 at her eye level. She didn't even know if she could tell any of her crew about this.

She realized that the clothes she had hastily pulled out of her bag included a new shirt that she had just purchased but had never worn. It was now being used to clean up her mess. She also lost her favorite shorts, which she was wearing. They were destroyed. She knew that she would never wear the new shirt again. She quickly donned the pair of sweats that she had also brought to this mortifying event. Now she was even hotter in the August heat.

She prayed that Jessie wasn't looking at the driver's side mirror and witnessing her misfortune. She opened the passenger door, and she was greeted with a shot of Lysol to the face. Jessie was spraying like a mad woman.

"Sorry," Sandy almost whispered. She was too embarrassed to even look her trainer in the eyes.

"You need my TA card for another shower?" her trainer asked, knowing the answer to the question. Sandy quickly grabbed Jessie's shower card, her shower bag, and some clean clothes and headed back inside, this time alone.

An hour and a half later, Sandy climbed inside the passenger's side of the truck and locked the door. The day couldn't end fast enough. Jessie was asleep, and Sandy quietly moved up the ladder into bed. Her stomach was finally quiet, but she took two more Imodium A-D pills just to be on the safe side. She would definitely not be eating any more Taco Bell. *What in the world was I thinking?* she chastised herself, still mortified and hoping that no one had witnessed her accident. Sleep finally claimed her, as the moon peeked through the crack in the curtain.

The next morning started like any other. Jessie didn't mention anything about the mishap. Even though she knew what had happened, she acted as if she didn't. Sandy didn't offer any information. She was just going to act like it had never happened. She was going to concentrate on finishing her training.

CHAPTER 18

BLACK ICE

The final push took Sandy and Jessie from California to Ohio. Once they dropped their load of produce off in Akron, Jessie asked for a load to run through the terminal in Springfield. The final trip to Springfield would give Sandy more than enough miles to complete the thirty thousand miles for her training, and Jessie would be picking up a new student and starting all over again.

Sandy had to give it to her Jessie. She was a fantastic trainer. She had learned so much in the six weeks that she had lived on Jessie's truck: FMCSA (Federal Motor Carrier Safety Administration) and DOT (Department of Transportation) regulations, running a legal clock, knowing how to use paper logs in the event of an electronic failure, checking in at shippers, checking out of receivers, and more. She learned how to distribute weight legally on her tandems, how to deal with weather conditions, and how to be the captain of her own ship.

She knew that she was far from being a seasoned driver but that she was on her way to being a great truck driver. She learned something new every day. The day that she thought that she knew everything was the day that she needed to hang up her keys and walk away from the industry.

Jessie told her once than once, "They will only know you're a rookie if you tell them." Sandy loved Jessie's offhanded compliments. She never came out and said, "Good job," or, "Nice work." But she would say little things, and Sandy took them to heart.

She had driven through some of the steepest mountain terrains and longest, straightest, and most boring interstates that this country had to offer. She had made it through some frightening storms by making decisions to pull off the highway and allow the storms to pass. She had delivered to plenty of rural receivers out in the middle of nowhere and to the heart of Newark, New Jersey, at rush hour on a Monday morning. She wished that she had more experience or training in winter driving. She finally got a tiny taste of winter on this last trek east.

Sandy was driving east on I-80 through Wyoming, and the weather couldn't decide if it wanted to snow or stay an icy mixture. Jessie had warned Sandy about black ice and always watching for spray coming off the back trailer's tires in her driver's side mirror. If there was no spray coming off the tires, it was not safe to keep driving, and she needed to find a safe place to pull over until it was safe to move again.

Sandy was cruising along at fifty-eight miles per hour, and spray was coming off her tires. The roads were relatively clean from early passes made by the salt trucks. She was approaching a slower-moving tour bus in the right lane, and she flipped her left turn signal on to pass.

Just as she started to pass the bus, she drove over a bridge. The bridge had patches of black ice, which Sandy could not see. She may not have seen the patches, but her truck and trailer felt and reacted to them. Her steering wheel jerked under her hands, and she immediately let off the gas pedal. She kept a tight grip on the steering wheel, and the truck and trailer righted themselves in the left lane as Sandy calmly took control of the situation.

She scared the shit out of herself, but she didn't panic. She apparently scared the shit out of her trainer as well because Jessie jumped out of bed, yelling, "I'm up."

"I'm up too," Sandy quipped, trying to make light of the scary situation. Jessie climbed into the passenger seat and remained there for the rest of Sandy's shift.

Jessie calmly talked about never passing on a bridge. Bridges were always the first to ice over, so she must be careful once the weather started turning bad. This was one of Sandy's biggest disappointments during her training. She was finishing up her required miles of training, and winter was officially still weeks away. She was heading into the winter season, and she would be getting plenty of experience in real time but without a trainer.

Sandy made it safely to the end of her shift. She was more than happy to pass the steering wheel to her trainer. She was mentally exhausted and bone tired. She had hoped to fall asleep immediately. But every time she closed her eyes, all she could see was her trailer sliding in her driver's side mirror, as she felt the wheels sliding on the black ice.

Jessie's shift was uneventful. She found a Walmart that allowed truck parking. She ended her shift in Iowa. Sandy was still sleeping. Jessie knew that she had scared herself to death and that she hadn't easily gone to sleep. Jessie parked, logged off the Qualcomm, left Sandy sleeping, and went inside to shop.

By the time she came out of the store a short time later, Sandy was awake and brushing her teeth while sitting in the passenger's seat. Jessie pushed her shopping cart to the passenger's door and opened the door. Surprised at what Jessie had purchased, Sandy leaned down as Jessie handed up a microwave. She then handed up a girlie purple bedding set and a little white rice cooker. Jessie then pushed the cart to the cart corral and climbed into the driver's seat.

Sandy had a puzzled look on her face, and Jessie said, "These are for you—for your new truck. You deserve it." Jessie caught Sandy off guard with her generous gifts, and Sandy wanted to cry but not in front of her trainer. Jessie wasn't a "huggy," mushy type of person, but Sandy was so moved by her generous gifts that she jumped out of her seat and hugged Jessie anyway.

"Aw, thank you, Ol' Stank Eye," Sandy said, trying to lighten the mood in the front of the truck. "I love everything. Thank you so much." This part of her journey was rapidly coming to an end. Sandy quickly secured her gifts on the top bunk and got ready to start her shift eastward. She couldn't wait to get her own truck.

***

The final hundred miles to the terminal belonged to Sandy. She was just as excited as the day that she had arrived in Springfield back in the summer and on the first day of orientation. But she felt like she had grown into a completely different person in the last four months. Even though she had been soul-searching before she had left home, without a doubt, she now knew where she belonged. That place didn't have a physical address, but it definitely had wheels beneath it. She loved her decision, and she didn't regret a thing.

She pulled into the terminal lot, turned on her hazards, stopped completely, blew her city horn, and slowly entered the inbound bay. This would be her last time in Jessie's truck. Next time she left the terminal, it would be in her own truck.

She pulled into the bay, parked so that the reefer motor, which was on the front of the trailer, was under the exhaust hood, pulled her brakes, and turned the truck off. Jessie was sitting in the passenger's seat, attempting to look nonchalant. But Sandy knew that this day was a proud one for her trainer as well.

Sandy raised her right fist, Jessie raised her left, and they met in the middle of the truck for a final fist bump. They had done it. She had done it. She was ready to upgrade and move into her own truck.

PART 3

CHAPTER 19

WASSUPP!

Three months after being alone on the road, Sandy felt like a true nomad. She didn't know if this was how other truckers felt, but she absolutely loved being a single woman with no family and home to go to. Of course, she had family but not one that she had to leave, as in the sense of the traditional trucker of old, who left his wife and kids for months at a time. Once he came home to his family, he was ready to get back on the road, his mistress (his truck), and the wide-open spaces of the country. She completely understood the pull. It was the siren song of the road. It was almost mermaid like, but it had the open road instead of a rocky shoreline and crashing waves.

Since she had left her home in early summer, Sandy had already traveled through forty-six states in the lower forty-eight. She had yet to take a load to or through Maine and Rhode Island. Her goal was to get to those two states at some point. But she couldn't complain about a thing. The life that she now led was incredible.

In the last month alone, Sandy had rearranged her truck multiple times. Just when she thought she liked the way she had everything organized, she would hit her head or reach for something and decide to move different items. She was determined to be the queen of organization in such a tiny space. After all, this was her new home. She had yet to go home, but she had made plans to celebrate Thanksgiving and Christmas with her family. She was looking forward to seeing everyone in a few weeks.

Simultaneously, her cell phone buzzed, and her Qualcomm dinged. It was new load information. Every time Sandy got new orders, she felt giddy. She never knew where she was going from one load to the next. It was exciting and thrilling.

Even her mom was excited for her as well. Her mom's first question daily was usually, "Where are you headed to next?" This was followed by, "What are you hauling?"

Being the funny girl that Sandy had recently brought back to life, she rolled with it. "What did the rabbit say before he ate his dinner?" Sandy asked when she was on speakerphone with her sister and her nephews. "Lettuce pray."

Her nephews giggled. They couldn't imagine a whole trailer full of lettuce, but they thought Aunt Sandy was super funny.

Now that she was out of training, Sandy invested in a nice Bluetooth headset and a window phone mount. She finally felt connected to the outside world. She spoke to her parents almost daily.

When her dad answered, he always asked the same question. "So you still like driving that big rig?"

"Absolutely," she would answer. Her dad could hear the smile in her voice.

Being grown and married, her kids called periodically. She was happy to get calls from each of them, but they had their own lives. She loved that they thought of her from time to time.

As of the previous week, Alex and Shrimp had both completed the TNT portion of their training, and now all five members of her crew were in their own trucks. The first time all five of the crew spoke to each other was one for the books.

Stacy had just called Sandy, and they were comparing their routes and schedule. Then they heard a beep.

"Hey, Sandy, hang on a minute. Lemme add Alex. She's beeping in."
"Okay."

"What's up?" Alex boomed, sounding happy and very grown up.

"What is up?" Stacy responded, as Sandy echoed with, "Sup?"

Then there was another beep.

"Hang on, y'all, Mahala is beeping on my end now," Sandy said while laughing.

"What's up?"

"Sup?

"Uppppppppp?" Stacy finished for Sandy's 'Sup' comment.

Then there was yet another beep.

"Hang on." It was Alex's turn to interrupt. "Shrimp is beeping in."

Shrimp boomed, "What's up y'all?"

All the girls responded at the same time.

"Wassupp!"

"Wassupp?"

"What's uuuupppppp?"

"Wasssuppp!" Each voice lent their own personal style to the phrase.

Sandy exclaimed, "Oh my God, guys, we are like that old Budweiser commercial with Charles Stone III."

Stacy and Mahala both laughed, knowing exactly what Sandy was talking about. Shrimp and Alex, however, were confused.

"What?"

"Huh?"

They both asked at the same time. They sounded as confused as hell.

"You know," Sandy explained. "Those guys answering the phone at the same time saying 'Wassup,' in the Budweiser Super Bowl commercial from the late 1990s."

Light bulbs seemed to go off.

"Oh, you mean the 'Yo Dooky, wassup,' from the *Scream* movie?" Alex says, laughing hysterically.

All five girls laughed hysterically. The age gap showed its face again. But this moment would also make it into Sandy's journal that night when she got done driving.

All five women talked for over two hours. All trucks were described in detail, along with the experiences that they had had their TNT trainers. Not one of their trucks was close to another. They were spread out across the country. Sandy loved it.

Sandy told the girls about getting left at a truck stop in the middle of the night in Kentucky. Her trainer had had no idea that she wasn't sleeping but was being mistaken for a lot lizard while wondering when her trainer would return to pick her up. All of the girls thought that it was hilarious and such a typical Sandy moment.

"Only you, Sandy, only you," Mahala said and chuckled.

She also told them about her pop and squat with the magical deer in the moonlight, only to find out a week later that it was nothing more than a deer farm for deer urine. The girls were rolling with laughter. Sandy swore a couple of them were actually crying.

Still laughing, Alex said, "Oh my God, let me tell you about my pee-pee story." The words pee-pee sent them all into hysterics again.

The larger than life Alex described her trainer as a super-slim and uber-quiet young black guy who didn't quite know how to deal with Alex's personality and overall dominate nature. One night while at a shipper, Alex and her trainer were in the truck for hours waiting for it to be loaded. They had backed into the dock. They had been waiting so long that Alex was losing the battle with her bladder, and she couldn't hold it any longer.

Some companies had facilities for drivers while others did not. This one was part of the latter. Alex's trainer suggested that she pee in a cup.

"Have you seen how big I am?" Alex asked him and laughed. She was quite comfortable with the fact that she was a big girl. "There's no way I can pee in a cup in that little space."

"Well, go outside on the catwalk," her trainer suggested.

Alex thought about it and decided, *What the hell*. She grabbed a bottle of water to wash off the catwalk once she was done and climbed out of the truck. It was pitch-black between the tractor and trailer, and her truck was sandwiched between two other reefer trucks. The docks at this shipper were tight, and there was less than two feet between the vehicles.

Alex ducked under the brake and airlines. She climbed up on the catwalk and looked around nervously. Feeling pretty safe in the pitch-black night and security of the truck fairings and side wings, Alex pulled her pants down for the quickest pop and squat in history. Then she quickly climbed down and poured her bottle of water over the catwalk. She looked around again. Seeing no one, she climbed back into the truck to wait for the shipper to finish loading her truck.

Three hours later, Alex got a call from the shipper, telling her that the shipment was ready and that she needed to go inside for her bill of lading. It was still dark out as Alex walked toward the shipping office. The driver of the truck on the passenger's side of her truck must have received the same call because he started walking toward the office too.

As they matched their steps, the other trucker acknowledged Alex, saying, "Great night out, isn't it?"

"Yes, it is," Alex offered.

"I think you have an issue with your trailer," the other driver said, looking ahead and not at Alex. "I think you have some type of a leak."

Mortified, she did not know if this driver had seen anything. "Ummm, I think my trailer was in defrost mode," she said. She quickly walked inside. She couldn't bring herself to look over at the driver. She was afraid of seeing a knowing smile. All she wanted to do was grab her paperwork and get to her truck.

Alex made it back to her truck and unleashed her emotions. All she could do was sit there and laugh. She woke up her trainer because she was laughing so hard. Once she told him what the other driver said to her, her trainer laughed along with her. She was ready to get out of this shipper's lot as soon as possible.

The girls loved Alex's story just as much as Sandy's. They continued to talk for a few minutes until Sandy's dispatch beeped in. All girls promised to call each other again soon.

Sandy finished the call with her dispatch and updated an appointment time for her delivery in the morning. She pulled into the nearest rest area so that she could look at her location and plan her required thirty-minute break and stopping point for a night with the revised appointment time. She loved the freedom of making her own decisions. As long as she delivered the product on time, she stayed in the good graces of her fleet manager and dispatch.

CHAPTER 20

FROZEN EYEBALLS

The holidays had passed, and Sandy entered the new year with a fantastic attitude and a new lease on life. She spent time with her parents, her children and their spouses, and her siblings and their families. Just like the truckers of old, after she had spent a week with her family, she was ready to get back in the saddle. The siren song of the road was quite strong.

She made the decision to lease her home out in the spring with the help of her son Mark. He lived close by and said that he would put all of her furniture into storage, once the winter cold had passed. She made this decision because she had spent less than ten days in her home in the last nine months. She could well afford her mortgage and other living expenses, but she wasn't there enough to enjoy the house. *Why keep paying a mortgage on an empty house?* she thought. If she rented out her home and put that money into her savings account, her nest egg would grow substantially.

Sandy was currently in Milwaukee, and it was beyond frigid outside. The weatherman on a local radio station warned of a polar vortex, which was a term that Sandy had never heard before. Living most of her life in the Deep South, winters remained mostly mild. A couple of inches of snow would shut the state down. A fourth of an inch of ice was a state of emergency.

Sandy soon found out that a polar vortex produced some extremely cold temperatures. It was negative fifty-two degrees worth of cold, according to her truck's outside temperature gauge. Sandy made it to a TA truck stop at the end of her shift and found a spot within walking distance of the building. Normally, parking further away and walking to the building was no big deal. She was working on eating and being healthy. Walking was something that she enjoyed doing. But the polar vortex made her look for the closest spot to the building.

By the time Sandy had bundled up, she oddly resembled Randy, the kid brother of Ralphie, the beloved star of *A Christmas Story*. With a thick winter thermal undershirt, long-sleeve T-shirt, hoodie, and winter coat on, she couldn't put her arms down. If her girls were there to witness such a funny sight, Sandy would have mimicked the scene of Randy's mother wrapping his super long scarf around his head, as his arms stuck out from his sides.

She caught a glimpse of herself in the door of the building as she approached. She had on a pair of fleece leggings under her sweatpants, two pairs of thermal socks, and her cute polka-dot rubber rain boots. Her MARI TRUCKING knit cap was hidden under a bright red plaid scarf, which her mother had given her for Christmas. No one item of clothing matched. She did not care, as she safely made it to the building. Her eyeballs felt as if they were almost frozen in their sockets.

She shuffled inside, dragging her feet and trying to knock as much of the dirty snow and ice chucks off of her boots as possible. The heat of the building was a welcomed feeling. She hadn't showered since the day before, and she was looking forward to a hot shower and meal at the restaurant attached to the truck stop.

She stood patiently in line as she waited for a shower ticket. When it was finally her turn, she asked for a shower. The cashier hesitated a few seconds, and then with pity in her eyes, she told her that the water pipes had burst due to the extreme temperatures and that there were no hot showers available. Disappointed, Sandy said, "Well, at least I can get a hot meal."

But the cashier gave her another sad look. "I'm sorry. The restaurant is closed as well due to no water." Sandy understood and knew that it wasn't the cashier's fault, so she smiled, thanked her, turned around, and trudged back to the truck.

All this work to get into this getup for nada, she thought, laughing into her scarf. *I should have invested in winter-proof goggles as well*, she mused as she climbed back into her truck. The heat of the bunk heater welcomed her home. She stripped out of the winter attire, put on her house slippers, and kept her T-shirt, hoodie, leggings, and sweatpants on. She definitely was hoping for a load to Florida in the morning. Chicken noodle soup and a peanut butter sandwich were on the menu for that night. Sandy picked *Cast Away* for her nighttime entertainment. *Tomorrow has to be warmer. It just has to be,* she thought.

Sandy didn't get a load to Florida, but she did get a load to Oklahoma. *Close enough*, she thought. It was time to thaw.

One of Sandy's favorite pastimes while on the road was listing funny and unusual names of towns, cities, streets, roads, rivers, creeks, road signs, and company logos. One of her favorite laugh-out-loud street locations was Clinton Drive in Houston, Texas. While Clinton was a pretty common name for streets, buildings, and landmarks in the South, while driving on Clinton Drive, she passed Fidelity Street and couldn't hold back her laughter.

She was talking to Stacy at the time, and she practically squealed, "Oh my God, Stacy, I just passed the corner of Fidelity and Clinton. I bet neither Bill nor Hillary could reside in this area," Sandy exclaimed, laughing way too hard at her own joke. Stacy wasn't nearly as amused as Sandy was at her joke.

One of the funniest signs she passed read in large white letters, "HITCHHIKERS MAY BE ESCAPING INMATES." The sign wasn't exactly funny and was quite common in areas where prisons were located near interstates. The thing that Sandy found hilarious was that a poor road-worn hitchhiker was using the sign as a leaning post for his break. His backpack rested on the dusty ground by his feet, as he leaned against the sign that warned of escapees with his thumb in the air.

Sandy managed to honk her air horn and laugh crazily as she drove by. She hoped that he would look up and see the reason that no one was stopping to pick him up. "Mother Trucker!" she yelled and waved as she passed. The hitchhiking bum didn't get the joke.

Toward the end of February, Sandy's phone rang at 3:00 a.m. She was in the middle of a good sleep, and she had set her alarm for 10:00 a.m. Her load wasn't due at the receivers until 2:00 p.m. Her phone lit up with Alex's name. Worried, Sandy scrambled for the phone. "Hello? Is everything okay?" Sandy asked, thinking the worst.

"Hey," Alex practically yelled into the phone. Sandy could tell that she was outside in the elements. "I'm having trouble with my tandem pins. They won't release, it's ten degrees below zero, and I'm freezing my ass off. Got any suggestions?"

Sandy sat up in bed, rubbing her eyes. "Okay, what have you done so far?" she asked, trying to help troubleshoot from afar. She could hear the howling winter wind through Alex's headset. She even thought that she heard her teeth chatter.

"I've poured alcohol into the air lines. I've pulled and pulled on the release pin, and it won't release," she yelled. "I even put my feet on the tandem bar and tried to pull the button out."

Sandy bit back a laugh as she pictured her poor friend with snot frozen to her face and her feet pressed up under the trailer, attempting to release the tandems. "Have you used the claw side of a hammer to try and pull it out?"

"Yes, I've tried that already."

Sandy suddenly had an idea. "What is the number on the trailer, Alex?"

"164520. Why?" Alex asked.

"Have you tried pushing the pin instead of pulling it?" Sandy asked, thinking about some of the 16-series trailers having a push pin release instead of the standard pull pin release. Sandy heard Alex pushing the pin and the whoosh of air as the tandem pins released.

"Well, son of a bitch," Alex cussed. "Do you know how long I have been out here in this icy shit?"

Sandy was laughing by this time, and she said, "You're welcome, Alex. I'll talk to you tomorrow. Good night."

"Good night, Sandy, and thank you."

CHAPTER 21

FLAT STANLEY

Sandy felt honored. She had just gotten off the phone with Oliver, her oldest nephew. He had asked her to help him with a school project. The class had read a book from the *Flat Stanley* series. The literary character had been flattened by a bulletin board and given powers to travel. Each student had been given a blank Flat Stanley to design and decorate in their own unique way. Then they were to give him to family and friends. Those family and friends were to document Stanley's journey with photos and mementos and to send him back to the student and the class.

Aunt Sandy was now responsible for keeping Flat Stanley alive and taking pictures of all the cool places that he saw. Oliver knew that Aunt Sandy went all over the country, and he was excited for Flat Stanley to join her. Sandy was going to have fun with this. Sandy's sister emailed Stanley to her, she printed him out, and off they went. The journey was fun, and Aunt Sandy chronicled their adventures for Oliver and his classmates. Sandy emailed Oliver's teacher, Ms. Meg, every Sunday evening and sent pictures of Flat Stanley visiting all over the country.

February 3rd

Dear Oliver and Ms. Meg,

Oliver, thank you for sending me to your aunt Sandy. She's awesome. But she drives a lot. We left Springfield, Missouri, yesterday. She drove through St. Louis, Missouri and then Illinois. I went over the Mississippi River, through Indianapolis, Indiana, and, and to Ohio, where we stopped last night in Groveport, Ohio. We were tired. We're going through Chicago, Illinois, right now, and we will be in Menomonie, Wisconsin, in two hours. I don't know where we're going after that.

Sincerely,
Flat Stanley

February 10th

Dear Oliver,

I'm tie-urd. Get it? Hehehehe. I'm tired man. You didn't tell me I'd really be seeing everything.

When we got to Wisconsin, we picked up forty thousand pounds of McDonald's fries and took them to Mason City, Iowa. I wanted to sneak into the trailer, but Aunt Sandy gave me the stank eye.

We then drove to Ida Grove, Iowa, and picked up forty thousand pounds of turkey. We have to be in Oakland, California, on Monday morning by 8:00 a.m. So by the time you go to class, I'll be close to the San Francisco-Oakland Bay Bridge and the Pacific Ocean.

We drove on I-80 through Iowa, Nebraska, Wyoming, and Utah and Nevada. We stopped in Salt Lake City. It was awesome. The Bonneville Salt Flats are neat, the mountains are huge, and I can't wait to see the ocean.

I'll write to you next weekend and let you know where I went. I've ridden over three thousand five hundred miles already. Thank you for my adventure.

Sincerely,
Super-tired-but-having-fun Stan the Man

February 17th

Dear Oliver,

Adventures abound, and I met my cousin this week: exhaust-Ted. Get it? I'm exhausted. Whew, let me tell you what happened.

We were headed out west and were almost to California when we got a call. We had to meet another trucker in New Mexico and trade trailers with him. His truck had broken down, so we had to take his load of raspberries and strawberries to Denton, Texas.

We went to Galveston, Texas, and we got caught in the middle of the tropical storm Imelda. Aunt Sandy had to wait almost six hours before she could drive. It was *still* raining crazily and windy, but we made it to the town at the southern tip of Texas called Laredo. It was right at the Mexican border. We were picking up a load of tomatoes.

We had to go through inspection, and they asked if we were US citizens and wanted to see our papers. Aunt Sandy showed her license, and all I had I was 'me'. I'm made of paper, so Aunt Sandy handed me over.

Long live the original Flat Stanley!

February 24th

Dear Oliver,

Hi, I'm Flat Stanley 2 (My picture is included in this email). Aunt Melissa printed me out and gave me some updated looks. I may look like a geek, but I know that my shoes are tied and that I can see better than the original Flat Stanley. Do you like my new glasses?

Just like Flat Stanley, I'm tired already. After leaving Laredo, we headed to Michigan with the tomatoes. When we got to Champaign, Illinois, we received a call. Another driver needed our help, so we had to take his trailer and head down to Georgia. I know how much your daddy loves the Detroit Lions, but we didn't make it to Michigan. I did wave, so please tell him that.

After we dropped off the load in Georgia, we got a load of Tyson chicken and headed to Delaware, Ohio. Do you want to know the name of the road? It was Pig Jig Boulevard. How funny is that? We just delivered to a Kroger.

Aunt Sandy drove us to Springfield, Ohio, to pick up some Dole fruit. Now we're heading to Pleasant Prairie, Wisconsin. I know you and your mama loves the Green Bay Packers, so I'll make sure that I wave. Aunt Sandy will start driving tonight because we'll have to be there by eight in the morning.

I hope you and your classmates are enjoying our adventures. If you see any big trucks on the road, be sure to wave or pump your hand in the air and listen for the air horn. You will make a trucker's day.

Sincerely,
S2

March 3rd

Good morning, Oliver,

I want to send you a quick letter while Aunt Sandy is sleeping. We are in Amarillo, Texas, and we are in route to Mankato, Minnesota.

We left Wisconsin last weekend and took a load of chocolate to Edwardsville, Illinois. We picked up a load of all kinds of Hershey candy bars. Before I could ask, Aunt Sandy said that if she couldn't sneak any candy bars, neither could I. I think she was reading my mind.

We took that load of candy bars to Springfield, Missouri, and then we went to Aunt Sandy's terminal to get the truck worked on. It was so nice to stop for a night, but it didn't last long. We had to get back on the road.

This time, we took forty thousand pounds of cheese all the way to Ontario, California. After that, we got a load of all kinds of vegetables from a Walmart distribution center in Colton, California. We are taking it to Minnesota tomorrow.

The southwest is awesome and so are the mountains. We had to take a southern route because there are big snowstorms in the Rocky Mountains and I-80 and I-70 are icy and snowy. We have to be safe and get all this stuff to the stores so that everyone can eat.

When we start driving today, I get to see some new states: Kansas and Minnesota. Guess what, Oliver? I heard that *you* are coming to Missouri for spring break and that we get to go on some adventures together. I'm stoked.

Eat some cheese and chocolate and study hard. I'll see you next week.

Sincerely,
Flatter-than-usual Stanley

March 10th

Dear Oliver,

I'm glad I got to spend several days with you on spring break, exploring the caves and the Discovery Center in Missouri. Do you remember the fun time that we had making new outfits for Stanley's next adventures and Dr. Stanley joining us at the Discovery Center? Well, I'm sorry to inform you that Dr. Flat Stanley is no longer with me. I apologize for his untimely demise. But when living on the road, it's a risk, and Dr. Stanley was brave until the end.

Let me tell you about his last two weeks of life. It was pretty eventful for us. We weathered tropical storm Olga in Mississippi and Alabama, with its torrential rains and high winds. Then we drove through Tennessee to pick up some frozen chicken, and then to Georgia and picked up two new members of the team, Oreo and Bella. They are two of the cutest dogs ever.

Bella loved Dr. Stanley, but he whispered to me that Bella had doggy breath. It must be the doggy biscuits that she loves to eat. We drove up to Washington, Indiana, and through the Hoosier National Forest in the middle of the night. It was very spooky. We picked up a whole truckload of turkey and took it to Iowa.

Once we got to Iowa, a late winter storm called Bessie came blowing in from Colorado, and we got snowed in for the night at the world's largest truck stop in Walcott, Iowa. That snow was blowing hard, and boy, was it cold.

The next morning was beautiful. I thought it would be a wonderful time to have a photo session with Dr. Stanley in his first snow. So I put tape on his back and stuck him to Oreo. Oreo is a responsible dog, right? I thought that would make for some really cute pictures.

I didn't realize how hard the wind was blowing and snowing. I picked Bella up and sat her on the ground, I turned around, and Dr. Stanley was gone. I panicked. I asked Oreo what happened to Dr. Stanley. Oreo said, "Who's Dr. Stanley?" I thought he was more responsible than that. I searched under the truck and under the trailer. I walked down the row of semis—all kinds of them. There was no Dr. Stanley.

Dr. Stanley and his white lab coat were practically the same color as the snow, so I guess you could say that he was camouflaged. I felt terrible. Poor Dr. Stanley was all alone in Iowa in the winter storm Bessie. He was such a brave, brave, brave flat man.

His legend lives on. It's a good thing that I have a printer and that Flat Stanley has lives like a cat because Spring Stanley will be making his debut soon.

I hope you and your classmates will have a wonderful week. Study hard and be good for Miss Meg.

Sincerely,
Aunt Sandy

Sandy had so much fun with Flat Stanley and loved emailing weekly letters and pictures of Stanley's adventures on the road. She loved getting the responses from her nephew and his classmates. Life on the road knew no bounds.

CHAPTER 22

I'VE GOT THE POO ON ME!

Sandy could tell that spring was in the air. She was driving through Amarillo, and the smell of cow dung burned her nostrils. "Whew," Sandy said, as she was talking to Alex on the phone.

"What is it?"

"These stinking cows," Sandy said. "It's almost as bad as my unfortunate poop fiasco in So Cal." This was the first time Sandy had ever mentioned that embarrassing event to anyone, and it had happened almost six months earlier.

"Oh, this sounds gooooood." Alex laughed, knowing by now that Sandy and her stories all came with laughter.

Sandy was already laughing. "Hang on. I have to pull over to tell you this story. If not, I may wreck my truck."

Sandy pulled over at the next rest area, logged out, and grabbed some yogurt from the fridge to eat on her thirty-minute break. She settled into her bunk and tried to retell the events of that fateful evening and the embarrassment that she had felt as she had barely made it to the shrubs. Alex was laughing like a hyena during the entire story.

"Oh my God, Sandy, you shit on an entire homeless community?"

"Wait, what?" Sandy said and laughed, just not as hard as Alex did.

"You said you shit on a homeless man."

"No, I said that I *could* have. Lord knows if anyone was living in those bushes. I was too embarrassed to look," Sandy said.

"Well don't feel too bad, girl. I have a shit story too. Oh, Shrimp and Stacy do too. You need to ask them about theirs," Alex said while laughing.

Sandy was intrigued. She had a smile on her face. "Okay, girl, spill it. It can't be worse than mine."

Alex took in a deep breath and began. "About a month ago, I met up with Matt, and I spent the night on his truck. I don't know if I told you that?"

"I don't remember if you did or not," Sandy said, knowing that Alex had just started dating a guy named Matt who worked for a competing trucking company.

"Well, I didn't have any food on my truck, so Matt gave me some tuna pouches that I could use for lunches until I got paid. But these tuna pouches were the hot buffalo flavored ones. Have you ever had them?" she asked, not waiting for Sandy to answer. "Well, I ate a pouch as soon as I got to the truck. It tasted really wangy, but I thought it was because of the buffalo seasoning. I never had it before." Sandy could hear Alex pull the brakes, and she knew that Alex had most likely stopped at a fuel island of a truck stop.

"I had a long night with Matt, so after eating the tuna, I went to bed. My load wasn't ready for me to pick up until much later that night. I go to bed, and girl, I don't know how long I was asleep, but I woke up with searing pains going through my guts." Alex was laughing and talking at the same time. She made an emphasis on the words *guts* because she knew it was on Sandy's bugaboo list. Sandy was laughing as well, knowing exactly where this story was going.

"I stood up, and I didn't even have time to open the door before I was messing up my pants. It was horrible. I didn't know what to do." Alex was crying by this time and laughing very hard.

"You remember in *Bridesmaids* where Melissa McCarthy and all the girls get food poisoning, and she ends up in the bathroom sink screaming, 'It's coming out of me like lava'? Yeah, that was me. I finished what I was doing, and then I stripped off my leggings and threw them away. I used so many baby wipes, just trying to clean up the best I could. Then I threw on some dirty sweatpants.

"I grabbed my shower bag and a set of clothes and walked as fast as I could to the building. I damn near yelled at the cashier that I needed a shower, and she looked shocked. I repeated myself. 'I need a shower, and I need one now!'" Alex yelled. Sandy laughed hysterically, visualizing poor Alex in distress.

"The cashier finally understood my urgency and handed me a shower ticket. As I walked to the back of the building, my stomach made the same gurgling noise that it did in the truck. All I could do was pray that I'd make it to my shower room." Alex was almost breathless now.

"My shower number was called as I walked down the hallway. I punched the code into the door, and I was on that damn pot, yelling like Melissa McCarthy's character, 'It's coming out of me like lava!' Yeah, I'm pretty sure everyone in the nearby showers heard me that day."

Sandy and Alex laughed and laughed. Sandy no longer felt so bad about her accident because her girl had a story to match hers. Her ribs and stomach hurt from laughing so hard. Oh, how she loved this. Alex and her poo were definitely making it into her journal.

"And you know what?" Alex asked, not waiting for the answer. "That damn tuna was expired." Sandy was almost breathless when she asked Alex about Shrimp and Stacy's story. "Hang on. Let me call them and click them in.

"Wasssupp," Stacy boomed, followed by Sandy, Shrimp and Alex echoing, "Wassupp," and, "Yo dooky! Whatttt's uupppppppppp?"

"Oh my God, y'all, I mentioned something about having an embarrassing poop story, and Alex said that you and she both had stories."

"What happened to you?" Stacy asked. Sandy repeated her So Cal, weeping-blue-spruce mortification. Laughter was crackling on all four phone lines. "So now that you know my horror story, it's your turn to share," Sandy told Stacy. "Alex said it's funny as hell."

"I don't know about that, but it's embarrassing as hell," Stacy said, beginning her story. "I was still on my trainer's truck when tragedy stuck," Stacy said, sounding very serious.

"It was in the middle of the night. We weren't under a load, and we didn't have to pick up anything until the next day, so I was asleep in the top bunk, and my trainer was sleeping in his bunk. I don't know if it was something I ate or maybe some type of food poisoning, but early in the morning, I woke up to searing pains in my gut." Alex and Shrimp cackled at the word *gut,* Sandy, however did not. *Guts is almost as bad as moist,* Sandy thought.

I didn't even have time to wake up my trainer to ask him to lower the ladder. I was having my own lava situation right there on the top bunk."

Suddenly Alex interrupted Stacy's story. "What in the actual fuck, driver! I know you see my big ass over here. Can't you read my mother-fucking turn signal?" Alex yelled at the top of her lungs as the sound of her turn signal could be heard in the background along with her air horn. "Get your ass to moving, or I'll move it for you. Dammit!" she threatened. "I'm sorry, Stacy." Alex's voice was suddenly calm and so normal that they'd never have known that she just had a violent outburst at another driver. "And you were saying?" she sweetly asked. The girls burst into laughter, all knowing the exact feeling Alex had just felt.

Without missing a beat and still laughing at Alex's outburst, Stacy continued. "I was so embarrassed. I just lay there. My pants were a mess, and I tucked my blanket around me, trying to keep the smell from coming out. My trainer slept on. I was sure he could smell it, but nooooooooooo, the bastard slept on. It started oozing through the tiny holes of my gym shorts. It was so embarrassing. I bet I lay there for an hour. Then I finally couldn't take it anymore, so I started hitting the window," Stacy rushed on.

"What?" Sandy and Alex asked at the same time.

"I hit the window by my head, hoping to wake my trainer. I wanted him to think it came from the outside like someone was hitting his truck, so he would get out of the truck."

"Ooooooohhhhhhhh," the girls said in unison, understanding what she meant.

"After hitting the window like five times, he finally woke up and asked if I heard the noise. I pretended to just wake up and said, 'Yeah, I think some dude hit your truck.' So he jumped out of bed, grabbed his phone, and rushed out.

"Once he left, I stripped down and balled up my blankets, shorts, and everything and threw them in a trash bag. I hit the showers. I had sprayed so many different types of Lysol and air freshener, I'm sure he was funked out of his mind when he came back to the truck. I stayed in the shower for an hour and then bought me a new blanket for my bunk.

"When I got back to the truck, my trainer was lying in bed watching TV. He acted like nothing was wrong, so I did too," Stacy said, finishing her story, as the other girls tried to catch their breaths.

"I've got the poo on me," Sandy sang out, quoting Joe Dirt, when the septic tank was strapped to his back. There was more laughter all around. These girls were too much.

"Well, Shrimp, you're up." Alex giggled and put her bestie on blast.

"Mine isn't as *explosive* as your guys' dooky dooky." Everyone laughed at the word *explosive*.

"Alex, you remember this one, dontcha? We were at the terminal, and I was cleaning out my truck back by the pavilion. I thought for sure that it was just gas." Everyone could see where this was going.

"And I didn't think nothing of it. I got done cleaning, and we headed in to eat at the North Grille. Chris, the guy who was sitting with us, asked out of the blue, 'Oh my God, Shrimpo, when did you sit on a chocolate bar?'" Everyone was cackling because they knew that it was *not* a chocolate bar.

"While we are on the subject," Sandy said, heaving and trying to catch her breath, "Kevin told me his embarrassing poo story." Poo was the funny word of the day.

Kevin was a fellow trucker that she had befriended online late one night on Facebook while asking a question about her truck. Kevin was ten years younger than she was, but he had been driving since he was nineteen, so he had a wealth of knowledge. Kevin had a plethora of stories, and many a night, he kept Sandy in fits of laughter.

"When Kevin was young, he teamed with his uncle. Usually, they always parked on the row that was the furthest from the building. His uncle had parked sometime during the night, so Kevin didn't know where he had parked or where they were. He got what he called the 'bubble guts.' I hate that term, but Kevin had it, and he had it bad.

He didn't think he'd make it to the building, so he jumped out the truck and dropped his pants and business on the ground. What he didn't realize was that it was 7:00 a.m., and his uncle had parked on the front row at a Love's truck stop." Sandy was laughing so hard that she almost couldn't finish his story.

"He pulled his pants up, finally looked up, and realized that he was the center of attention and embarrassed beyond belief. He quickly climbed back into the truck and yelled for his uncle to wake up and that they needed to leave—now!" Everyone was dying laughing. "His uncle called out from behind the curtain, 'You shit in front of the ladies, didn't ya?'" There was more laughter.

"That's pretty shitty," Alex quipped, and the girls laughed until they wiped the tears from their eyes.

CHAPTER 23

LASTING MOMENTS

Every day, Sandy wrote something down. She didn't care if it was something simple like writing details about MARI TRUCKING, the Salt Lake City Terminal, or the boat that was on top of a dilapidated garage in a hoarder's paradise, in the middle of nowhere.

Sandy's daily journal entries grew. She came to the conclusion that Utah was her absolute favorite state. The Moab area on US-6 was her favorite road to travel. She also decided that the tunnels under Boston ranked at the top of her bugaboo list. She especially ranked it at number one and in all capital letters if her GPS lost its signal while she repeatedly looped through those tunnels under the city.

Pretty moments made it to her journal as well. One such place was a trip to New Berlin, New York, for a load of yogurt. The snow came down heavier than it had been predicted. Sandy was able to maintain a slow pace, even though no snowplows had made an appearance. New England was absolutely gorgeous in the rural parts but extremely aggravating in the urban areas.

On this late afternoon in particular, Christmas lights shone from every house. Sandy thought she had gone back to an earlier time like the 1940s. Everything looked so magical. Her hazards were on, and she was traveling about twenty-five miles per hour. Huge snowflakes collected on her windshield.

In the opposite direction, she saw an Amish buggy, which was hitched to two horses, approaching her. In the back seat of the buggy, three little children sat all bundled up, complete with bonnets and pageboy caps. Three little gloveless fists came out from under their blanket and pumped wildly in the air. Sandy hesitated a fraction of a second, not wanting to spook the horses. Then she pulled on her air horn. The children's face lit up with glee. The mom glanced back at her children. Like a knowing mom of any child, she was not surprised. The dad, as any typical dad, remained stone faced, and he didn't quite enjoy the exchange as much as Sandy did. But that didn't take away from Sandy's magical moment.

The Amish children weren't the only children to make it into Sandy's journal. A few days into her training with Jessie, there was a broken-down minivan on the shoulder of the road in Kansas. Sandy signaled to move to the hammer lane (the left lane) and away from the minivan on the right shoulder of the highway. Two little girls stood behind their mom. Both girls began to jump up and down and pump their arms wildly. Sandy obliged by pulling on the horn a few times too many, earning an, "Is everything okay up there?" from Ol' Stank Eye in the back.

The memory that made her laugh the loudest was the group of Boy Scouts who were stuck on the side of the road, down in the heart of Texas. Topping a hill, Sandy saw a wrecker working on a van that had an enclosed cargo trailer attached to it. In the grass and well off the road, about fifteen boy scouts stood. All fifteen put their fists in the air and pumped them up and down. The thing that made Sandy laugh out loud was their adult chaperones, who had their fists pumping in the air as well. Sandy made every face split with a grin. Her smile stayed on her face long after she had passed that remote roadside event, which was near some sleepy little Texas town.

Magical moments could be found everywhere. In California, she witnessed not one but two dust devils spinning on top of Tejon Summit, which was on I-5 and commonly referred to as the Grapevine. She was traveling south and maintaining a safe speed despite the wind gusts, when she saw the twin funnels of dust spinning wildly on the eastern side the highway. Magical didn't even describe the moment.

Early on, Sandy decided that when she documented her journeys, she would document the bad along with the good. She documented wrecks that were terrible, horrific, and sobering. Some left her heartbroken and with the knowledge that the driver had little chance of survival. Animal deaths hit her hard as well. She had yet to hit a large animal, such as a deer, but she did claim a very large tortoise as a victim and felt miserable about it for hours.

In Vermont on a snowy day, she witnessed a dead deer on the edge of the road. Just as she passed it, she saw a magnificent bald eagle perched on the carcass. It was an unforgettable site.

Moments of pride also made it into her journal. The sight of an American flag flying at half-staff for the death of a former president or in memory of 9/11 brought a sad smile to her face. When she saw large flags hanging from fire trucks, which had their ladders fully extended, she felt pride for her country surging in her heart.

Sandy wrote about the different types of drivers who converged on the highways, all with the same sole purpose in mind: moving America's freight safely down the highway. She saw tall, lanky, young men with long legs, who, in two quick movements, jumped inside their trucks and were ready to go. Meanwhile, short and somewhat wide girls like Sandy took four times as long to climb into their trucks. People of all ethnicities and sexual orientations drove every day, and Sandy still couldn't seem to grasp how she had missed all of this before her life-changing decision.

There were girls who dressed up with full-on makeup, high heels, and fingernails. Then there were girls like Sandy, who were cute and neat in appearance but fresh-faced and makeup free. Of course, there were the female OG's (Original Gangsters) of the industry, who'd been there since the beginning. Those ladies reigned supreme in Sandy's eyes. It was a pot shot of which drivers were friendly and helpful to the new talent, and which drivers looked down on the new ones just beginning their careers. The responses ran the gambit, but Sandy treasured the talks that she had with other friendly drivers on the road.

As she had surmised in the beginning, there were fat, tall, short, and skinny drivers on America's roads. Some drivers were bigger than she was, and they seemed destined to remain so, as they chose endless fast-food meals and not much activity. There were also health nuts, who took time at the end of their shifts to walk or use the front of their trucks to do upright pushups. Sandy didn't exactly fit into either category at that moment. She didn't eat fast food on a regular basis, but she wasn't at the point where she exercised every day when she was done driving. She made a promise to herself that she would do much better.

Life on the road also came with confrontation. Sandy had one unpleasant experience at a truck stop in the panhandle of Florida, which she would never forget. She had delivered a load of produce and found a truck stop to stay at for the evening. When she got up the next morning and went outside to inspect her truck and trailer, she noticed that her windshield, grill, and headlights were coated in bug guts. Sandy hated driving in swampy areas, especially at night. The bugs were everywhere. When she was finished inspecting her truck, she drove to the fuel island to fill the truck and trailer fuel tanks.

Once she had inserted the gas-pump handles into the tanks on each side of the truck, she picked up a squeegee with a long handle and proceeded to scrub her windshield and headlights. She was intently scrubbing one of the headlights when she heard someone behind her cussing.

"Bitches like you are the reason we can't have nice things around here." Sandy heard the man, but she didn't bother looking over her shoulder. She wondered whom he was yelling at, but she didn't stop scrubbing.

In a louder octave, she heard the same voice say, "Bitches like you are the reason we can't have nice things around here." This time, Sandy stopped scrubbing her headlights and turned to look at the man who was yelling. It turns out that he was yelling at her. Between her and the CDRT truck at the next fuel island, a very slim and short old trucker with a porn mustache stood glaring at her. Sandy was surprised that he was yelling at her. She glanced around her to make sure that she was the source of his ire. She made eye contact with the CDRT driver, who was fueling his truck and watching this situation unfold between Sandy and Slim Jim.

"What did you say to me?" Sandy asked, her face getting red. She wasn't scared, but he did catch her off guard.

"I said it's bitches like you that are the reason we can't have nice things."

Sandy was baffled. "What in the world are you talking about?" she asked calmly, trying not to make the situation worse.

"You fucking using the squeegee on your headlights. What do you think you're doing?" Slim Jim barked, pointing his finger toward Sandy's headlights.

During training, Sandy was taught to always wash the headlights of road grime or debris whenever she stopped for fuel. That was part of maintaining her truck. Her face started to get hot. She glanced over at the other driver who was fueling and then looked back a Slim Jim. She calmly turned her squeegee so that the squeegee part was close to the ground and the end of the long handle was close to her face.

She said, "I'm washing bug shit off my headlights so I can see tonight when I drive. I'm washing glass headlights, not tires or the engine compartment like I see so many drivers do." The more she said, the madder she got. "I suggest you mind your own business, or I'm going to shove this stick in your suck hole." She surprised herself with what she said, but she didn't back down. "Have a good day, asshole," she said and then turned around and finished cleaning her headlights. She held her breath, hoping he wouldn't do anything to her. She slowly exhaled as she heard him walking away.

She finished cleaning everything, put the squeegee back in the bucket, and proceeded to remove the fuel pump handles from the tanks. When she made eye contact with the driver next to her, he was laughing hysterically. She felt embarrassed. "Why are you laughing?" Sandy asked and then started to giggle nervously.

"I was worried when I saw him walk up to you, and I was afraid I was going to have to defend your honor. But you, little lady, need no help."

Sandy laughed and asked, "What is wrong with people?"

The driver shrugged his shoulders and laughed. "You're guess is as good as mine. Keep the sunny side up and the rubber down," he said as he climbs into his truck. Sandy waved and finished what she was doing.

Once Sandy got back on the road, she called her friend Kevin and told him about her tangle with the asshole trucker. Kevin listened as Sandy described everything. The he asked, "What was he driving?"

"I don't know. Some type of older model semi with a car hauler."

"Was it a Long Nose Pete?" Kevin asked, referring to the old boxy style model of a Peterbilt.

"Matter of fact, it was," Sandy confirmed.

"What was he wearing?" Kevin asked.

"Ratty Wrangler jeans and an old faded T-shirt. He had a big belt buckle," Sandy replied.

"Was he wearing fingerless gloves?" Kevin inquired.

Sandy didn't know where he's going with the conversation, but she confirmed that he did have on fingerless gloves.

"Sandy," Kevin said while laughing, "that wasn't an asshole trucker. That was a *super trucker*!" Sandy laughed along with him. "Welcome to trucking, darling," Kevin drawled. "This won't be the last run-in you'll have. But I'm glad you stood your ground."

Sandy was proud of herself as well. "Exactly what did I do wrong?" she asked Kevin.

"Not a damn thing," he replied.

The more she drove, the more she enjoyed the solitude at the end of the evening or morning, depending on when her day ended. She was getting good at cooking and preparing simple meals in her truck. She had weaned herself off carbonated beverages before the holidays. She was on her way to becoming a healthier, happier Sandy. She felt good and comfortable in the skin that she was in.

She had found her laughter while she was in night school. It was still in her eyes and soul every day. She found funny whenever she could. Salty or sweet, humor came in all forms. She was walking out of Walmart with supplies for her truck when an eighty-year-old scruffy-looking man walked in wearing a shirt that said, "WILL WORK FOR SEX." Sandy laughed all the way to her truck and seriously wondered if the shirt produced any promising leads for a job.

She loved coming to the top of a hill in farm country, the wide-open prairies, or deserts with many huge wind turbines. Those turbines initially overwhelmed Sandy, especially at night when they were all lit up with blinking red lights. They reminded Sandy of an alien ship landing to take over planet Earth. She sent a photo text of a line of wind turbines, which went as far as the eye could see, to Sinclaire. Sinclaire's response made Sandy giggle. He said, "Wow, Mom, look at those pinwheels."

On a bright, sunny weekend, she was driving through Kansas. The road was an endlessly straight highway, and running parallel to the highway, there was a railroad track with a train hauling turbine blades on it. The train and the road seemed to go on forever. The blades were positioned back to back on the flatbeds, giving the impression of large sets of angels' wings. The view was incredible.

The craziest thing that she had to endure on the road and that was echoed by her girls and other female trucking friends was pervert assholes. Sandy would get a glimpse of some asshole trucker passing in the hammer lane. He wasn't there to pass her quickly and get back into the right lane like he should, but he was matching Sandy's speed so she was forced to look at what he was doing. Naked from the waist down, his junk in his hand, and with a dumbass look on his face, the pervert trucker found pleasure in the shock and disgust on other trucker's faces.

The first time Sandy experienced it, it completely shocked her. As she talked about it with others, she realized that there were plenty of men out there who thought everyone needed to see what God had given them. Her friend Rosie told her that when something like that happened to her, she'd roll down her window, laugh, and yell, "Is that all you got?" They would quickly drive on.

So far, Sandy hadn't done more than glance. When she quickly realized what was happening, she didn't look any lower than his chest level. She realized that if she slowed down completely and let a few other trucks get between her and stubby, it made the situation better for her.

Sandy tried not to let the bad days of trucking affect her. It was a hard job. It could be stressful at times when she had to deal with tires that needed to be replaced, had to call roadside assistance for issues with a trailer, she was late, or a shipper cancelled a load. Dealing with cars and oblivious drivers who darted in front of and around her at any given time was the worst. She tried to counter every bad incident with something good.

Her love of the road outshone any bad moment that she encountered. When she saw two water towers in a small town, one that said, "HOT," and one that said, "COLD," it made her day. Going through the small town of Trenton, Tennessee, and seeing "31 m.p.h." signs made her giggle.

Driving through I-40 in Arkansas and seeing an "Adult XXX" store sign next to a local sign for McDonald's gave the impression of an adult McDonald's. *Who wouldn't want to eat at an adult McDonalds?* Sandy thought and giggled. Every day, Sandy added to her journal and her growing number of photographs about life on the road.

CHAPTER 24

FRIDAY THE 13ᵀᴴ

Winter seemed to last forever, and in some northwestern states, Mother Nature had reared her ugly head well after the first day of spring. Sandy was positive that she had driven through every winter storm.

She started out the winter season skittish as a newborn calf. Many a night, she would find a truck stop at sundown and plan on driving at dawn's early light. Her first run-in with black ice was still fresh in her memory. As each storm system came into view, she grew stronger and felt better about driving in snow and an icy mix. She still had yet to use chains on her tires. *If the weather is bad enough for chains, I shouldn't be driving anyway*, she reasoned.

"Standing on the corner of Winslow, Arizona. Such a fine site to see," Sandy sang as she passed under a Winslow, Arizona sign on I-40. "There's a boy I love in a flatbed Ford, slowing down to take a look at meeeeeeeeee."

Sandy and Stacy were on the phone as usual. It was unusual for the two to go more than three days without talking. When they did go three days, it was because one of them was driving nights and the other days. There were a handful of times when both girls ended up driving all night and getting to their receivers for a 3:00 a.m. or 4:00 a.m. delivery. They had become the best of friends.

Today was Friday the 13th. Sandy was not a superstitious girl, and she never had been. The same could not be said for Stacy. Sandy was hauling a load of milk out west on I-40 while Stacy was down at a cold-storage facility in southern Georgia. Stacy had spent three hours waiting to be unloaded, and her clock was slowly ticking down. She only had an hour window to find a truck stop or rest area to start her ten-hour break.

Sandy was cruising through Arizona, and she was telling Stacy about the wind and tumbleweeds that were making her nervous. "You know what today it is, right?" Stacy asked.

Sandy rolled her eyes and said, "Yes, scaredy-cat, I know what day it is, and no, scaredy-cat, I'm not letting the day affect me."

"Well, you get off that highway if those winds get too bad," Stacy lectured like an old mother hen.

"Don't worry, momma," Sandy cooed and laughed at Stacy's mothering.

"Okay, brat, don't make me get the belt."

Stacy heard a knock on her door and told Sandy to hold on a second. She opened the door and took the bill of lading from the dockworker. "Well that's service with a smile," she said to Sandy, as she started her truck's engine. "I didn't even have to go in to get my bills. They brought them out to me." She started her tractor, pulled forward far enough to shut her doors on her trailer, so that she could head to the nearest safe haven to end her shift.

Still on the phone, Sandy heard Stacy walk to the back of her trailer. Stacy, the scaredy-cat that she was, whispered what she was seeing as she walked to the back of the trailer. There was a thick, heavy fog flowing out of the trailer. It was caused by the difference between the icy cold ten-degree air in the trailer and the eighty-degree temperature of the Georgia heat.

"Girl, you should see the fog pouring out of my trailer. It's almost scary," Stacy whispered loudly. She got closer to the back end of the truck.

Sandy moaned like a ghost, "Woooooooo," and laughed.

"That's not fucking funny," Stacy yelled as she reached the back of the trailer, and fog completely enveloped her in the process. "It's so foggy, I can't see if there's any product left in the front of the trailer or not," she exclaimed, just as icy drops fell off the wind chute in the top of the interior, making striking noises like something sinister was inside.

Sandy teased, "You know what today is," repeating what her friend had said to her twenty minutes earlier.

"Not today, Satan, not today!" Stacy practically screamed as she slammed the doors, latched both of them, and slid her padlock in place. "If Jason or Freddie is stupid enough to climb in, he will be there tomorrow when I get the trailer washed." Sandy laughed all the way down I-40.

The next morning when Stacy drove to the truck wash, the trailer was empty and monster free, much to Stacy's relief. Sandy couldn't wait for the next crew call, as she now thought of it, so that she could tell the others about the day Stacy tried to trap Jason and Freddie on Friday the 13th in her trailer. It was another story she would add to her journal. Sandy made it safely through the tumbleweeds and the wind, and the milk was delivered on time. Stacy didn't trap any monsters, and they lived to haunt another day.

The other girls were MIA for the week. There were several weeks when their schedules just didn't sync. Mahala had been mulling the idea of teaming up with another female driver, and Shrimp and Alex tossed the idea of teaming together for the summer. *That will be an interesting team*, Sandy thought.

Sandy had been thinking a lot about training. She didn't know if she wanted a student on her truck for fifty thousand miles, which was the new company requirement. She wasn't sure that she had enough experience to do what Jessie did. She wondered if she would be able to wake up or stay wake through her student's shift and still manage to drive her own shift. She didn't think that she could. But she did love the idea of the MSD phase of training. MSD trainers took the student straight out of orientation. Their job was to teach the student everything she learned in night school or everything it took to pass the CDL exam.

A student typically took two-to-six weeks to train. One thing that had stuck with Sandy since day one of arriving in Springfield on the previous summer was the need for more female instructors. MARI TRUCKING had the highest number of female employees in the industry, but they needed more.

She loved the time that she had spent in night school, and she was thankful for the opportunity that they had given her. She also knew that the reason she had landed in night school was because of the lack of female MSD instructors. Plenty of male instructors taught female students, but if students requested female instructors, they had to wait several weeks, or they had to be accepted into the night program, which was a longer alternative.

Sandy planned on discussing the topic with her fleet manager in a few weeks when she would be in Springfield for the gala. The gala was an annual event meant to celebrate the women of MARI TRUCKING. She was looking forward to the glitzy, glammed-up event, which the owner spared no expense. She had already informed her dispatch that she needed to be routed into Springfield for the gala. She hadn't said anything to her fleet manager about training just yet. She was hoping the conversation would go the way that she wanted it to.

She also hoped all of her crew would be able to make it to the gala. She missed her girls so much, and she couldn't wait to see each of them.

EPILOGUE

Sandy was on her way back to Springfield. Excitement was building. She had ordered a dress and heels online, and she had a vintage turquoise necklace that her mother had given to her at Christmas of the previous year, which would pull the entire outfit together beautifully. Sandy loved looking cute on the road. She did not wear the typical ratty T-shirt and sweats, but this gala was giving her the opportunity to dress up and be a lady. She could not wait.

While she hoped that the entire crew could make it to the event, the jury was still out on Stacy and Shrimp. Alex and Mahala had already requested their dispatch to route them to Springfield. Shrimp and Stacy were still running hard out on the road.

She sent a message to her fleet manager requesting a meeting once she got into town. That meeting was scheduled for the morning of the gala. Sandy had discussed becoming a trainer with each of her girls, and each one gave her encouraging words. They all thought she would make a great MSD instructor, and she hoped her fleet manager would feel the same way.

Once Sandy made it to Springfield, she planned to rent a small storage unit for several things that she had in her truck, in the event that she was approved to become a trainer. Then she would need to make room for a student. She even mulled over the idea of relocating to the Springfield area in the future, if she qualified as a trainer. She no longer went home. Her son Mark and his wife, Amber, had rented out her house to a new tenant a few weeks earlier.

She was able to surprise her parents by coming through town with a load several times. She planned to see her oldest son, James, and his wife, Penelope, in California, the next time she went through the southern portion of the US. Sinclaire and Deshawn were expecting their first baby, a little girl, and Sandy was ecstatic. She was looking forward to being a grandmother trucker. Her family was used to her nomadic lifestyle.

She spent her spare time documenting the countryside. She had thousands of pictures from the coast to coast, although Maine and Rhode Island still remained elusive. She was tossing the idea of writing her first book around in her head. She had several journals and so many funny stories, which she added to every day.

She had had the courage to change her life almost a year ago, and she was thankful that she had. She couldn't imagine her life without living on the road. Maybe she'd have her first book published soon. After all, it was never too late.

Made in United States
Orlando, FL
08 April 2022

16611274R00088